THE PERFECT PAYBACK

By the same author

My Imperfect Love Story

THE PERFECT PAYBACK

SHUBHASHISH KERKETTA

Srishti
PUBLISHERS & DISTRIBUTORS

Srishti Publishers & Distributors
A unit of AJR Publishing LLP
212A, Peacock Lane
Shahpur Jat, New Delhi – 110 049

editorial@srishtipublishers.com

First published in India by
Srishti Publishers & Distributors in 2024

10 9 8 7 6 5 4 3 2 1

Printed and bound in India

Acknowledgement

Before anything and everything else, I would like to thank the Almighty for giving me the strength to complete this novel.

I would like to express my deepest appreciation to my mother Argen Kerketta, my wife Priya, my sister Yognisha and the little wonder of our life - my son, Sparsh for the unconditional love, support and blessings that they have been bestowing on me since forever.

Special thanks to R (you know it) for helping me through the days of frustration and blocks, for reading my shitty drafts and giving me invaluable inputs to make it better.

Heartfelt gratitude to my friend, who trusted me and shared a grey fragment of his life and helped me with this book.

I am highly indebted to all my friends who had been by my side and helped me knowingly and unknowingly throughout the journey.

Much obliged to Arup, Stuti and the entire team of Srishti for showing faith in my work and being wonderful right from the beginning to hone and present The Perfect Payback to the world.

And finally, I would like to thank all of you who are holding this book in your hand for the love and motivation that you have been showering on me.

Happy Reading!

Prologue

Ten-year-old Suyash, gazed towards heaven with a heart that was overflowing with rage! He walked in through the unlocked door, wiped his tears and mud-spoiled face with his palm and looked around hurriedly. His exploration ended as he caught sight of the axe that seemed to call him out raucously. A sinister smile clenched his lips as he walked towards it slowly, but unwaveringly. He picked up the axe that had been sharpened just a day before by his very own Bhuvan uncle.

He then dragged the weapon into the room, where the psychopathic monsters lay serenely after annihilating the child beyond reparation. His body shook vigorously and sweated profusely as he ogled at his prey and the axe in a row.

He did not waste a second further. Disgust and fury fuelled him sufficiently as he shouted at the top of his voice and struck Akki's neck with whatever residual strength was left in him. Blood gushed out immediately, but he did not yell. The man was tanked entirely and Suyash hit him repeatedly until the head fell off!

He then sauntered to the other side of the bed, where Bhuvan snored unconsciously without an iota of hint of what had happened or what was about to recur. Suyash screamed yet again and repeated the gruesome act.

Something had gotten into him... It was the demon that carried the purest form of hatred! The demon that pushed him to punish them for all the abhorrence they had made him undergo.

And then, he did not stop just there. He got on the bed and started hitting their dead bodies until the gizmo slipped out of his delicate, torn and blood-stained hands!

The bodies of Bhuvan and Akki had sixty-three cuts apart from the blows to their necks!

The kid then tottered to the other room and sat down, shakily gawping his blood-spattered face, hands, and body. The brash quiet of that dreaded night was crammed with his earth-shattering wails, "Mama... Papa..."

PART – I

Present

Full to the brim

28 January 2019, Raipur
(Saturday, 04:30 PM)

The doorbell rang and Kanika rushed excitedly to get to the door. She had waited enough and was going to get a glimpse of Suyash after five days, ten hours and sixteen minutes. Every minute of those days had been like a decade without him. But no more!

She unbolted the superbly designed door of her flat and was spellbound to see her man standing tall in khaki chinos, a white polo t-shirt and Aviator sunglasses. The suitcase stood beside him, proudly pronouncing its association with the owner.

She jumped and clung to him like an infant monkey, "I missed you so much."

The firm, muscular and sturdy six feet physique of Suyash did not move even by an inch due to the impetus. He hugged her back tight and replied, "I missed you too."

They kissed for the next few minutes in the corridor. There were three more doors on the same floor, but all those flats were empty; which meant that they could have continued like that forever!

"Are we only going to kiss after so many days, babe?" Suyash winked.

"It's okay if you only want to do that for now!" Kanika tried to turn the table teasingly, while still clinging onto him and rubbing her nose against his, "I can understand; you might be tired."

"You aren't that fortunate, babe! My endurance level is like there." He said, pointing towards the roof.

"I know all about it." She got off, caught his collar and pulled him inside the spacious two-BHK flat in Nava Raipur.

"You are driving me crazy already." He said as she pushed him onto the plush sofa and put her milky white legs on his thighs.

"I have something special for you," she said and started lifting her red floral dress.

They had done it a zillion times, yet he was captivated each time. A broad smile spread across her lips as she saw him gazing. Her man was hers and he was starved, being away from her for that many days. The only glimpse he got of her was during the late-night video chats that did not last more than twenty minutes.

The two were famished for one another and filled each other's cups to the brim that evening, until their bodies surrendered!

***

Kanika Chetri, Assistant Manager, Human Resource Department of RSM Steel Private Limited, was posted in Raipur, the capital city of Chhattisgarh, less than six months ago, after undergoing a two-week induction training in Mumbai. She got placed while pursuing her MBA at IIM Kolkata with a package she could have never denied!

Although, the stationing did come as a shocker! She had opted for and expected a metropolitan city, preferably Kolkata.

She was not enthralled about relocating to Raipur. However, she didn't have a choice! Things were grim, and she had already painted a dingy picture of the place in her mind, even before smelling its soil.

The location however, surpassed her bated breath! She had expected nothing, but a small village-type town filled with low lives. She had also imagined coming face to face with some Naxalites in some weekly marketplace while purchasing veggies, but what lay in front of her enchanted her – the ultra-modern infrastructure and staggering city life!

That was a significant relief to her and she conveyed the same to her parents, who seemed cool, a cool that was beyond acceptable! Kanika did not know then that the *beyond acceptable cool* was the thing that would reveal itself only with time.

Things had bypassed her apprehensions (in a positive way) initially, but it is a widespread truth that time has wicked ways of tricking us. The moment we think that things are sorted, we are proven wrong.

It happened that way with her! All the company flats in the area of Raipur were pre-occupied and she was the only one allotted a living place in Nava Raipur or the New Raipur area: the planned city that the government was developing to replace Raipur as the capital city.

Her excitement declined exponentially by the time she reached her flat. The place seemed more or less deserted. Most of the houses were empty. There were hardly any shops around and she did not find any public mode of communication. It did not take her much time to understand that the new found project still needed much time to reach its goal.

The place sucked, but she had no other choice.

"You will manage easily Kanika." She used to mutter to herself.

That sentence, however, lacked the conviction to the likes of ninety-nine percent. Kanika had no idea how she would manage things alone in an alien location that was itself alienated!

To her relief, the company provided her with a special cab and a driver, which came in extremely handy in that area. He used to come early in the morning and leave only after she permitted him to.

However, things went from bad to worse with every day that passed. Loneliness haunted her miserably and her efforts to find a companion went in vain. All the potential girls around her already had accommodations according to their requirements!

She gave up after a couple of weeks and started investing most of her time in the office. The practice put her in the company's good books within the first couple of months of joining, but weekends continued to be a challenge. The only way she found to combat it was by bringing in enough work home to keep herself busy for the next two days.

Then again, as it is said, change is inevitable; Kanika became a faithful witness to the same. The very same place and the flat that she had cursed innumerable times in the first three months of her stay transformed into a paradise the day Suyash set foot in her life and further on that floor.

Suyash had come into her life and had become akin to a drug more addictive than cocaine or methamphetamines! A stranger, a complete nobody, became her world within a brief span of two months. But this is how life designs things – strangers become soul mates and soul mates become strangers!

The past few days had been physically and emotionally overwhelming for her. She had never experienced that kind of *hard-core* love in her life. He had suddenly become an irreplaceable companion to her. A type of companionship that she had always craved, but had never dreamt of getting. He was the last person her eyes painted the picture of before dozing off (usually after a mind-boggling body-shattering carnal sex session) and the first person she saw before seeing anything else the universe had to offer! That was the first time in that many days that Suyash had gone out for an official tour that long.

Kanika had never imagined being that helplessly dependent on anyone, leave aside a man she had met just a few days back! She was one of those thick-skinned girls who made herself absolutely immune to the disease called 'love' and the carriers of the same called 'boyfriends'. It was that rock-solid commitment to her career, coupled with a relentless focus that helped her crack the CAT examination in her first attempt and get an enviable job through campus placement.

"Who needs boys? I want to be free of all this *jhamela* and I am more than happy with my girl companionship." That's what she used to say to Ruchi, who had been her best friend forever!

Her boy-allergic attitude, hilariously started inviting proposals from girls. There was once a time when she even accepted one during her grads (just for fun)! The news spread like a wild forest fire in the college and while her known group of friends deserted her, a new group of homosexual and bisexual girls started increasing proximity! All that aside, things got out of hand when her mom raised questions about her orientation! There was a giant mayhem and she was highly disturbed.

She had always been an outstanding student who consistently found herself in the list of toppers, except for the mentioned 'one semester' during her grads where she scored in the lines of fifties. But, being the smart girl that she was, she learned quickly, worked hard in the succeeding semesters to make up for the losses and never walked in that direction ever again. What followed after was rock solid focus, eminent success and the latest entrant, Suyash!

Yes, I drink!
Is there a problem?

11 November 2018
(Sunday, 08:00 PM)

That was the first weekend since Kanika had joined her office in Raipur that she decided to pamper herself 'coz one of her colleagues, Sweta, who had accompanied her to the office cafeteria on Friday told her, "What is the use of all this money Kanika, if you don't even take care of yourself." She was probably hinting at Kanika's naturally disintegrating and uncared hair and nails.

Kanika took her advice pretty seriously and booked an appointment for a salon and spa service.

She reached the place on time and enjoyed to the fullest as several girls cosseted, making her feel on top of the world. She left the salon fully rejuvenated.

She then went on a shopping spree, purchasing cosmetics and dresses for home and office.

"Take me to some nice bar!" She said to the driver while putting the packets on the car's back seat and stepping in. Although she was not that much of a drinker, it had been quite some time and that day seemed perfect to do all the stuff. She wanted respite from her boring weekend curse!

The middle-aged cab driver, who had just started accelerating, turned around immediately and asked surprised, "Where, ma'am?"

It seemed as if Kanika had asked him to drop her at the gates of hell. She was highly offended by his reaction and said, irritated, "Keep your eyes on the road and take me to a bar." The next moment she was frightened. His reaction made her doubt whether any other driver would take her to the place she wanted.

"Oh! Ok, ok." He said while trying to compose himself.

Kanika heaved a sigh of relief when he asked, "Madam, you drink?"

"Yes!" She said irritated, "I drink. Is there a problem?" She tried her best to keep her voice soft and conceal her exasperation.

"No!" The driver seemed to be a gentleman who realised that the conversation was heading in an unwanted direction. He apologised, "Sorry!" and said hesitantly, "It's just that I don't know many ladies who drink!"

"It's okay."

What followed next was minutes of burdensome quiet that reinforced her idea of getting herself relocated to any other place in the world.

Last one!

11 November 2018
(Sunday, 08:30 PM)

After some twenty-five minutes of tongue-tied drive, he stopped in front of a swish double storied building. He pointed towards the first floor and said, "Its' the best in town."

Kanika looked upwards towards a big flashy red board that read, *The Last One... Bar, Disc and much more...*

The place radiated a lot of much needed good vibes!

Even though she was indignant and repulsed by his point of view; she appreciated the fact that he had dropped her at some good place safely. She walked towards her destination with the packets in her hand through the mild crowd of youngsters as the taxi sped away.

That was the first time that she was going to get a drink all by herself and that too in an unknown city! Had it been Siliguri or Kolkata – the places that she was well-acquainted with – things would not have seemed that strange. However, she was there and then there was no turning back.

She paused to give it a second thought before stepping in through the big, heavy, red door that was guarded by a hefty gentleman, whose muscular body was highly discernible, even through his formals! A few of them in the same black and white uniform moved around the vicinity of *The Last One...!*

The loud music inside bypassed all the layers of sound proof walls and that big door allured her to get in. The intensity of the invite increased manifolds whenever someone opened the door. "It would be rude to step away now." She said to herself bathed by the irresistible temptation to get some of that ill-tasting spirit into her parched body.

One of the gentlemen in uniform understood her dilemma. He reached out and said, "Ma'am, you can step in without any hesitation. You have nothing to worry about with us around." He even took the packets and gave her a token before opening the door.

The placidity and reverence in his tone gave her the much-needed shove and she darted in while giving him an appreciative smile.

There are a lot of times when we want someone to push us to do something that we want to do, but lack the required courage and/or motivation. Moreover, that also gives us an opportunity to say, "I did not want to go, but was forced to." As silly as it may sound, it happens a lot and that was just one of those times for Kanika.

She moved through the crowd and deafening music while covering her ears trying to look for a seat. It took her some time before her senses adjusted to the sky rocketing energy inside.

The dance floor was filled with young guys and gals who were busy dancing at the beats of some hard music that the DJ had put on demand.

She scanned throughout and walked straight towards the counter, "Three tequila shots please."

The person was unable to hear because the music was suddenly turned louder and shouted, "What?"

She pointed the same on an oval-shaped wooden menu that seemed to have been carved out by *The Flintstones* from a tree trunk using some Stone Age tools. He smiled and signalled, "Two minutes."

That was one of the heaviest menu books she had seen with less than ten items engraved in a square foot of wooden tablet!

Kanika's general view about the people of that area started taking a U-Turn as she gulped in the alcohol and saw the uncaring crowd having the time of their lives. There was no gender inequality, no biasness, no chauvinism! Soon, she started falling in love with the place and the people as the colourless spirit mixed with her spirit!

"That was just one male chauvinist pig! An old-headed *languor*... Huh!" She said to herself, "But he did drop me here safely. Sorry driver *saheb*." She continued talking to herself as intoxication filled her veins!

"Hi." A male voice took her out of the trance.

She turned around to see an unknown face fixed on a sturdy six feet physique. He looked pretty handsome in those colourful flickering lights, or maybe it was the alcohol doing the job! The music did not seem to be that loud after those three shots.

She looked around to see if that 'Hi' was meant for someone else. She found but a few guys around, spellbound in their own world of booze and bees.

That clearly meant it was intended for her. She wanted to assess the situation before responding, but the liquor had already taken control, "Are you talking to me?"

"Yup."

"Do I know you?"

"Nope."

"Do you know me?"

"Nope."

"Then why the hell are you talking to me?" She almost yelled.

"Because I am alone and it seems like even you can use up a good company."

"Oh, but I like my solitude!" Kanika said and shouted sloppily, "Twwwo more shots pleassse!"

"But I want to talk to someone, if you may." The guy insisted.

Kanika had lied about being alone. She wanted to talk to someone. As a matter of fact, she wanted to talk to someone desperately. Especially after getting some alcohol in, she loved to talk.

The stranger had come as a saviour, but she had to ensure that he did not find her desperate. It should be the other way round. Only a girl can let that thought remain unaffected through intemperance!

"One large Black Dog, on the rocks please," he said to the boy who brought drinks to the counter in front of her.

She gulped in the fourth shot and squeezed a lemon in her mouth to shake the burn-off.

"Please," he said after a few seconds. Waiting for her to regain her composure.

Then when it was evident – even in front of the man at the counter who did not give a fuck – that he was desperate. She decided to bless him and said, "Okay! But I want to finish my drink first."

"Yeah sure." His face displayed contentment and she was happy at successfully veiling her want and make him look desperate.

Stranger walk!

Marine Drive, 11 November 2018
(Sunday, 09:15 PM)

"I never knew before today that Raipur has a Marine Drive!" Kanika's voice was still slurry as she walked alongside him on the red and yellow tiled pathway on Marine Drive.

"You need to learn a lot about Raipur!" The man smiled.

That place was a five minutes' walk from the bar and was swarmed with people even at that time; quite contrary to what she had expected! Young couples enjoyed their togetherness under a million stars and a cool breeze; groups of carefree teenagers relishing the best days of life and numerous old people who were probably out for a walk after dinner, discussing politics and glaring social issues with each other. She was amazed to discover a small town with that kind of nightlife. Nobody cared what the other person did. Just 'her' kind of life!

The broad pathway was built between a small lake and one of the busiest roads in the city! The place was finely lit and had wooden and cemented benches to sit; most of which were occupied! A lot of hawkers moved around with *chana jor garam* and *mungfalli* apart from various food stalls of *golgappe, chaat, dabeli* and popcorn.

Kanika made a mental note to hang out in that place all alone. It seemed extremely cool, but right then she had the company, of course, of a complete stranger!

"So, what's your name?" He initiated the conversation after they walked silently from the bar to Marine Drive and then a few steps again.

Kanika was busy enjoying the tranquillity and was completely unaware of the words spoken by him. She felt an untainted peace after combatting the deafening noise in the bar! It was only when she had stepped out that she realized how stressed she had been inside!

"Thank you!" She responded in her trance.

"What?" He asked with a smile. He knew that she was lost in the serenity that the spot offered at that time.

"I mean, thank you for bringing me to this place." She clarified.

"It's totally my pleasure, as a matter of fact I should thank you."

"Why?"

"Because, you agreed to give me the much-needed company"

"Hmm... You are welcome," she said with a victorious smile.

"So, you didn't answer my question."

"Sorry! Can you please come again with it?"

"What's your name?" He asked again.

"Oh! I am Kanika and you?"

"Hi, I am Suyash." He said while putting forth his hand for a shake.

"Is it an excuse to touch me?" She said with a smile while looking at his hands.

"No, no. It's just a force of my habit," he said and withdrew his hand immediately.

She laughed and said, "I was kidding" and put forth her hand for a shake that he took unstintingly.

That was just a couple of months back when she first met him before he became her world!

Immaculate

Suyash used to work for MNB Bank Ltd., one of India's largest private sector banks, as the Marketing Head of Central India, who reported directly to the National Head in Mumbai!

Kanika had helplessly started to develop feelings for him soon after their first meeting in the *Last One,* which matured rapidly with time. Moreover, she didn't think there was a girl who would not have been victimized by his charm. He had an impeccable personality, looks to die for and an acute sense of humour. Furthermore, he was an extremely well-behaved human being with an immaculate taste for everything, including his drinks. The best part was that he always had time for her, despite his hectic schedule. That alone made her feel far more than extra special! Even when they were bleakly chained to work, the two eventually found themselves linked to one another. Their days began and ended with each other. They met practically every day unless one of them was unable to do so. And that miss was amply made for by the eagerly anticipated weekends (the same weekends Kanika used to despise during her early days in Raipur), which flew by in the blink of an eye! "Does he feel what I feel?" Kanika often asked herself. It was evident that he was all into her, but she could have never been sure unless he told her.

She wanted to be sure, but was not even vaguely prepared for what was about to transpire! As a matter of fact, she wasn't prepared for anything that life was going to serve her in the days that followed!

08 December 2018 (Saturday, 07:15 AM)

Kanika's eyes opened to an unknown apprehension that made her spring up and sit on her bed at once.

"Damn! Did I oversleep?" She asked herself nervously because she did not want to be late for the movie date that had been in their to-do list since the beginning of the week. She checked the time hurriedly and sighed in relief as the phone said, "07:15 a.m." Her alarm was due in the next fifteen minutes.

Suyash's official tour had proscribed them from seeing each other for the last three days and Kanika did not want to waste even a second more. She was super excited for the meeting after long days of loneliness. She switched on the data of her phone with a smile on her lips; knowing his messages would be waiting to slip in. That had become a routine and she did not even need to check the phone to ascertain it. His daily routine was on her finger tips! He was an early bird; got up every day at five and never forgot to text her before heading towards the gym.

"Gudmng"

"Have a gud day"

"I am sorry but we will have to drop today's plan"

Three messages flashed in simultaneously.

All her excitement vanished like a mirage in the desert the moment she saw that last text from Suyash! She threw the phone on the bed in disappointment and then picked it back up in less than a second.

Something very urgent might have come up! She tried to make herself understand. There was no point in making an issue out of it. Moreover, they were not paired up until then and she didn't believe she had the right to fight with him over that!

She took some deep breaths and composed herself before replying to all of them as maturely as was possible for her.

"Gudmng"

"U too"

"Okay... No problem...!"

The day became meaningless to her at the start. She was extremely annoyed and had no idea how she was going to spend the next forty-eight hours of her life.

"Aaaaagh!" She rubbed her head in disappointment and said, "You are taking him way too seriously Kanika. Maybe he doesn't have any feelings for you. Stop thinking so much."

"Get out of my head. Get out of my head!" She repeated those words again and again while wriggling on the bed before dozing off again!

Take my hand, take my whole life too!

08 December 2018
(Saturday, 8:21 AM)

An unexpected knock at the door startled her not-so-deep sleep. "Who the fuck would come at this hour?" She thought angrily looking at the mobile screen that said, "8:21!"

For a moment she had considered it to be her imagination until she heard it again.

"Ufff!" She murmured irritated and went to take the door.

"Who's there?"

A soft voice from the other side said, "Courier service ma'am!"

"Who the hell sent me what?" She thought and peeked through the peephole to find a guy dressed in an orange and white T-Shirt that said, "EHS Couriers." The person had a small backpack on his back and was holding an envelope in his hand. His face was buried towards the floor. All she could see was the orange cap. That was definitely a courier service guy who was nearly sticking his nose into the door blocking every other view.

Must be a new guy with a lack of etiquette. She thought and opened the door.

What happened next was nowhere in the purview of her mind's eyes. The view outside gave her a mild heart attack and her legs turned shaky immediately!

"Oh my god!" She said covering her mouth with her hands.

The courier guy stepped out of the way giving her a clear line of sight. The whole area, both the walls and the floor were exquisitely decorated with hundreds of bouquets and pots of beautiful flowers: pink, yellow and red roses, white lilies, zinnias, colourful carnations, gerberas, peonies, sunflowers, tulips and plenty of other flowers.

The whole entrance resembled a *paradise on earth*. The charm of the set up was enhanced manifolds as three white rabbits tagged with red ribbons on their necks hopped around through the spaces between the bouquets and pots.

"This is soooo cu...!!!" She was saying when the timeless romantic song by Elvis Presley started echoing in the entire stairway!

Wise men say, only fools rush in
But I can't help falling in love with you
Shall I stay? Would it be a sin
If I can't help falling in love with you?...

The exquisiteness of the ambience was miles away from her prettiest dream and she was thoroughly enchanted. She looked around clueless, trying to make sense of everything when the rabbits started moving around and licking her toes.

She bent down to caress and reciprocate the affection that they were bestowing on her and caught sight of the golden capsules that were dangling on the ribbons. She touched those shiny egg-shaped pods with quivering fingers enquiringly when a voice inside warned her meekly, *Just stop. I don't think it's for you Kanika.*

She, however, chose to ignore it. Curiosity overwhelmed her as the rabbits sat down comfortably in front of her. It was evident that they were trained not to jump away when she reached for the cases!

"The capsules will detach easily if you pull them out, ma'am." The courier guy shouted to override Elvis Presley's voice. She followed the words with no attention to him.

Soon, the three golden capsules, approximately two inches long that had a joint at the centre, shone in the midst of her palm and the rabbits started jumping around once again.

"You can break open the cases from the middle, ma'am!"

All of this was happening while the music continued and she followed the voice again. She got three golden papers from inside that had 1, 2 and 3 written on them.

She opened the first one that said, "I."

The second one, "LOVE."

She had already guessed the word in the third paper, "YOU..."

Blissfully confused, she turned towards the courier guy and uttered the words that she had been wanting to since the beginning, "What is this? I think you came to the wrong address!" She was sure that those were meant for someone else and that there had been a big mistake.

However, a giant tsunami of emotions shook her vehemently as the guy got down on one knee with his gaze fixed on to the floor and lifted a bright red rose towards her.

"What the hell? Who are you?" That was the first time that she had turned her attention towards him.

The guy removed his cap, lifted his head and looked straight into her eyes with a victorious smile.

"Oh my god, Suyash!" She shouted at the top of her voice, feeling absolutely stupid to have not recognized him until he chose to reveal himself!

"Yes, Kanika... I love you!"

She was elated, embarrassed, surprised, shocked, on top of the world and dumbfound, all at once! All she did was to stare at him motionless as drops of tears rolled down her cheeks uncontrollably.

Suyash looked at her confused and said apologetically, "I am so..."

"Shhhh!" She hushed and hugged him tight and replied, "I love you too. I love you very much Suyash!"

A new beginning

29 December 2018
(Saturday, 4:45 PM)
Cafe Coffee Day, Raipur.

"There is something I wanted to ask!" Suyash said while sipping his all-time fav mocha.

Things had been unbelievingly beautiful for the brand-new couple drenched in love. Three weeks had passed within a blink of an eye and every moment was bliss.

"What is it about?" Kanika asked, slowly churning the costliest brownie known to her. The taste was however worth every single *paisa*!!!

"I want to be near you all the time. I want to see you first as I open my eyes and last when I doze off at night. I want to hug you whenever I want and wherever I want. I want to...."

His unremitting *'I want to's'* were inadvertently interrupted by a sudden attack of hiccups that made the pieces of those sumptuous eatables fly out of her mouth frenziedly. She tried to veil her embarrassment by covering her mouth and turning her back towards the man, but Suyash acted extremely cool. He signalled one of the waiters to bring a bottle of water immediately.

The singlets were nothing but a bad reaction to something Kanika had presumed. She had anticipated that he was about to propose for marriage and she wasn't even remotely prepared for that.

The uninvited hiccups pushed some of those dry brownies to the most sensitive parts of her throat and made her cough uncontrollably, adding to her woe! The bottle reached soon and she gulped it in a single breath.

"Are you okay?" He asked worriedly after a few seconds while rubbing her back.

"Yeah, I am so sorry." She replied trying to hide her face from him. She looked around speedily to assess the amount of humiliation she had inflicted on herself.

"Aaaaah!" She let out a long sigh of relief as she saw everyone around busy in their own sweet world, or that was what everybody made her feel so in unison.

"It's okay Kanika! You need not feel mortified. It's quite natural and can happen to anyone anytime."

"Hmm... Still..."

"Forget about that." He said after giving her a few more seconds to relax, "I was in the middle of asking you something."

"Yes, you were saying..." Kanika said while swallowing a big lump in her throat.

"I just want to stay with you all the time."

She leaned forward towards him and asked doubtfully, "What do you mean?"

No... no... not marriage... She prayed in her mind while thinking about all the polite words to reject his proposal.

"I mean... I want... I mean..." He stammered.

"You are making me nervous Suyash!" His nerviness added to hers in multiples of thousands!

"No... I mean... " He paused for a sec, let out a deep breath and said, "Okay! Let's shift together."

"Oh! Thank god!" Kanika sighed in her head.

It was not as bad as she had assumed; yet doubts crept into her mind. Although, she wanted to be with him all the time, she had never thought in that direction.

"Do you mean live-in?"

"Yup, kind of, but with commitment," he said while still looking down at the table. He evidently had a lot of doubts in his mind too!

"I have never considered that option and my parents are too conservative." Kanika spilled her heart out. The proposal had ignited inexplicable excitement within her, but she also had numerous apprehensions that seemed to take the reigns.

None of those trepidations in her mind were unique. It was all that is common to everybody who is new to a relationship..

"Only if you are comfortable honey." He said lovingly while keeping his palm on hers, looking straight into her eyes for the first time in the past six minutes, "You can take all the time you want!"

"Hmm... Let's do it," Kanika said perfunctorily because she knew that she would turn it down if she gave it a second thought.

However, the picture of her parents, relatives, neighbours and various caretakers of the society started flashing in front of her eyes. She even picturized her father approaching her with a big knife, eager to cut her heart out!

"I think you should think it through the night Kanika. It's not an emergency." Suyash said after reading her facial expressions!

"No, I don't want to think anymore. I want to stay with you. I don't want to be afraid anymore. Moreover, nobody is going to come here and check. I know a lot of my friends who stay with their boyfriends. So..." Kanika said in a single breath. She said those words more to herself than to him.

"So?" Suyash asked.

"So... When do I get to shift?" She asked.

"Actually, I was thinking if you could allow me in to yours." He replied with a childlike innocence and the smile that always hit the right chords in her heart!

"And why would Mr Suyash want to leave his five-star rated luxurious flat and move in to my humble dwelling? Don't you want me to enjoy the best-in-the-world facilities with you?" Kanika asked bewildered.

She genuinely did not find a good reason for him to renounce his lavish company, provided accommodation that was located in one of the poshest areas of the city with all the five-star facilities. The campus was equipped with all state-of-art amenities. and was a whole new ultra modern world inside.

"Because it is devoid of an imperative requisite!"

"And what's that?"

"Privacy, Kanika. You know that the place is brimming with all kinds of families with senior citizens and kids and they would definitely not regale an unmarried couple in their vicinity. You know the stereotypical norms of the society!" He smirked.

Suyash had a valid point. Kanika had been to his place a couple of times and had turned uncomfortable at the number of eyes that scanned her inside out. He was one smart individual thinking in the right direction.

"So, when do you want to come in?" She asked immediately.

"Tomorrow."

"What? Really?" Her eyes went wide open!

"Yup, why waste time when we have already decided the course of action." He winked.

"But, my flat is a mess and..."

He interrupted her and said, "Don't worry baby. We shall *un-mess* it together.

"Okay, as you say." She replied half-heartedly, unable to find anything else to say after a few seconds of silence. Things seemed to be happening too quickly, but she decided to go with the flow!

Was that a right decision? Only time would reveal!

Black Sheep

Things got settled at a whimsical pace after Suyash shifted to her place.

Kanika decided not to tell her parents about her new live-in setup, but Suyash shared everything with his family and it was exceedingly shocking for Kanika to find them least bothered.

"You have the coolest parents!" She concluded after a five-minute video chat with them on the second day. His mother was a rather chirpy woman and she became friends with her immediately. Although, Suyash's father did seem austere, as expected, but was responsive and tolerant!

"Really!" Suyash replied with a sarcastic smile that left Kanika guessing. She, however, did not give it that much thought then.

Time however, slowly unclogged the unseen and she was surprised to learn that he was the *Black Sheep* of his family. It was kind of impossible for her to believe that a highly successful and intelligent person like him could be unwanted.

The fact is that even the blackest sheep in an average Indian family is accepted as the whitest and most adorable after the kind of job Suyash was in! Nonetheless, every black sheep has a story. A story that explains how a cute, innocent and an extremely loved child suddenly becomes redundant in a family.

In Suyash's case; the story had a name – Manisha.

She was his girlfriend from college and they had sustained that relationship for four years until he got a job and was posted outside his hometown of Fatehpur in Uttar Pradesh. Unfortunately, Manisha belonged to a family that was in constant conflict with his family over land possession issues from twenty years ago. The news of their relationship was akin to detonating a ticking time bomb that shattered his life. He had a heated squabble with his parents, especially his father and uncles, as they prepared for a war against Manisha's family! He stood in front of them, leaving them no option but to gulp in their fuming anger. Suyash, however, paid the price and was disowned by everyone and was thrown out of the house immediately!

Manisha, who was offered the same choice by her parents, had differing reflections and she chose her family over him!

* * *

On one of those evenings, Suyash spilled his heart out to Kanika regarding the tragic incident that followed and changed his life further for good! He started narrating,

Just two days after I was driven out of my family, Manisha called me and said, "I am sorry Suyash, but we cannot carry on."

My heart felt a heavy thump the moment those words hit me. It had never occurred to me before that she would dump me like that. Moreover, I had never thought that that was the last time I was hearing her. My voice was asphyxiated, "But why Manisha... What happened?"

"I am the only daughter and I cannot leave my parents for you." She said coldly, as if I had a dozen brothers and sisters.

She disconnected the call with a bang before I could have said anything else. I tried calling her back immediately and then a hundred times afterwards, but she went out of reach.

I even went to her house to persuade her, just to be beaten and thrown out of the area. That was when I saw taciturnity in her eyes

and realised the cold truth: It was over!

Those were the nights when I slept pressing the pillow against my face to avert the sound of my painful wails to leave the periphery of my bed. The awful twinge in my heart coupled with absolute loneliness had turned my life into living hell.

Days passed as I immersed myself in an ocean of things in search of peace and distraction. I worked overtime, gambled, drank and then drank again while ingesting a lot of smoke. Nothing helped!

I wanted to talk to my mom. I wanted to sink into her lap and cry. But she was nowhere around and all of it was my fault. I chose a fucking perfidious girl over her. I had fucking ruined everything.

On one of those crestfallen evenings, I was walking back towards my flat with a bag full of grocery items and my mind and body that were overburdened with alcohol, weed, desolation and dejection. A speeding car emerged out of nowhere and hit me in the middle of the road. I have no memory of how I had toured from the pavement to the middle of the road in my trance. I did not hear any of the multiple shouts and honks; as I was conveyed. The only thing I remember was seeing a pair of bright lights that ran right through me with a loud thud!

The next time when I opened my eyes it was in a hospital bed. I had been unconscious for five long days as I was told. I had suffered severe concussion, fractures in my left arm, ribs and shin bone, ligament tear in my left knee and multiple cuts and bruises on my entire body, including my face!

I was in intense pain, but all of it faded the moment my eyes caught sight of mom staring at me. She was in close proximity to me after months and her eyes proclaimed the wariness, the care and the love noisily. It was evident that she had not had a proper sleep for a really long time.

I had been yearning for her and started wailing the moment she caressed my forehead. She joined me right away. She had missed me. I could have told that may be much more than I had missed her; after all, she was a mother. Moreover, she might have never thought of seeing me in that condition; all broken, wounded and bandaged and that for sure was an unwarranted affliction on her!

"I am so sorry mom." The words struggled through my strangulated throat.

"Don't talk son; it will hurt!"

The pain and love hidden in the words exhibited intense struggle and intricacy.

All she cared for even after everything I made her go through was my comfort; and I had decided to choose a fleeting love over her. I hated myself, but made a solemn promise that very moment, "I will do everything to keep her happy."

I still thank god for the accident. I think that is what everybody calls a blessing in disguise!

It restored my family; at least a part of it. Of course, things were not like before; my dad and uncles ensured the same, but I hope things will get better with time!

He still believes that me choosing a girl over family was a mistake that I would have to pay by never stepping into that house. He even took away my right to cremate him or even be anywhere near his dead body. I pray he lives after me!

Thankfully, he had no objection over me talking and meeting mom outside the periphery of 'his' house.

It was only after my mom's multiple efforts that he agreed to see you, his bahu, that day. She had told him that the two of us got married after her consent!

"Whoa! Come again! What did your mother tell your dad?" Kanika lost all interest in his narration immediately and was shocked at the price at which her supposed father-in-law agreed to see her.

"It's nothing Kanika." Suyash tried to convince.

"What nothing! This is unacceptable Suyash." She said rigidly.

All the sympathy that had built up in the last few minutes was replaced by exasperation.

"I am sorry. I just wanted to make things right with my family." He replied with tears in his eyes.

"And you didn't think it necessary to at least tell me once." Kanika shouted.

"I didn't know mom would say so Kanika. I never told her to." He said, "Moreover, I love you Kanika. I know it wasn't right on mom's part, but she did what seemed right to her and I had no problem even if you told your parents that we were married. I can see my whole life with you."

"It's not about that Suyash. You fucking won't understand!" Kanika shouted.

She had a whole legion of doubts and a hurricane of dander in her mind! Suyash tried to induce and pamper Kanika until late night, but nothing worked. She was utterly exasperated!

***

Kanika, however, did not know that Suyash had added the *bahu* portion, in that conversation with an intent to enhance the sentimental and the sympathetic flavour of his narration; and yet again he had not expected it to backfire!

Kanika's reaction had made it evident that he could not rush through the things. He understood that his impetuosity may put everything at risk. Furthermore, a single unthoughtful sentence followed by a reckless elucidation could result to an undue postponement of his well laid plan. After all, there is always a price to pay!

Nonetheless, he also knew Kanika; he knew that she wouldn't be able to hold on to her ire very long and he was right. He upped his efforts extensively to make good for everything. He brought gifts, flowers and her favourite chocolate almost every day; apologised a zillion times and didn't stop; sent her cute love messages throughout the day and continued talking to her sweetly even when she retorted indifferently.

Soon, his endeavours started working its magic on Kanika and she started enjoying all the attention and pampering from her boyfriend. She decided to stretch it a bit more even though all her anger had evaporated. Things, however, took a different turn on one of the evenings when Suyash brought a stick, put it in her hands, bowed down and requested her to vent out all her anger on him.

That was way too much and Kanika was conquered by guilt for her behaviour immediately. She threw the damn stick away and hugged him tight with tears in her eyes and nothing remained to be sorted out after that; just as Suyash had thought.

Recreating the first

12 January 2019
(Sunday, 9:00 PM)

"Shit! I think I already drank too much." Kanika murmured while massaging her temple. She did not want to lose control over herself before they even started.

It was a Sunday and the couple had decided to relive the first day of their meeting in the place where it all began, *The Last One...* as strangers! Suyash came up with the idea to *recreate the first* after watching some movie. Kanika backed the notion whole-heartedly because it not only seemed perfect to rejuvenate their relationship, but also ignited an enigmatic excitement!

Kanika sat on the counter just like the first time and ordered a vodka when Suyash darted towards her in his inexplicable swag (something that she had definitely missed the first time). She was mesmerized as he walked through the crowd in his black polo t-shirt and light blue jeans. His tall and sturdy structure bypassed all others in the place.

I was so stupid, I love him and yet I was fighting him just because his mother made me his wife in front of his father. Isn't that what I want? Yes, that's it! I want to be his wife. I want to be his. Now and forever! Her head was filled with those voices roaring at a sharp ten thousand decibel inside her head.

She was turned on just while looking at him as the colourless vodka continued adding colours to her thoughts and make her sway. She wanted to hug him right there and nothing kept her away from him, but their plan and the thrill of the unknown that was bound to slot in at any point of time.

She looked at him dotingly as he sat on the fourth high stool on her right and ordered a bourbon. She had dressed in a purple short dress and high heels and glanced cursorily at her reflection on one of the shelves at the corner of the counter before the two pairs of eyes looked at each other from the corners. Both of them realised that it was easier said than done: to enact being a stranger to a person whom you know and love!

He got up and sat right beside her after a few minutes and said, "Hi."

"Hi!" She replied and looked away immediately.

"I am Suyash!" He said and put his hand forth for a shake.

She waited for a few seconds before taking it and said, "I am Kanika."

"Wow, beautiful name!"

"Oh! Thanks." She replied and gestured the bar tender for another.

"Can I buy you a drink?"

"Why? Do I know you?"

"You have started to and you will know more with time."

"That was so lame! Sorry, not interested." Kanika sneered.

"Please no...I don't know what else to say."

Kanika started laughing outrageously the moment those words hit her ears. She was filled with inexplicable love as she saw Suyash standing beside her like an innocent child looking at her with pleading eyes.

"You are so cute! I love you so much," she said and hugged him tight.

Their plan to recreate the first day transformed into a complete debacle, but they were already on their way to create new memories; memories that were set to be relished by Kanika for some time before pushing her towards the path of regret and mayhem!

10:30 PM

"Just don't puke in the car!" He said with a smile while caressing the steering of his new Audi that he had bought after exchanging his old car!

"As if!" Kanika sneered derisively and big drop of tears started running down her cheeks immediately as she breathed in forcefully to avoid the mucous spill off her nostrils. Alcohol was running the show for her!

Suyash hit the brakes surprised and asked, "What happened?"

"You think I am boorish." She started sobbing, "You don't love me!"

"No babe..." Suyash was able to sweet talk her to stop crying after minutes of struggle.

He then handed her a couple of tissue papers that she used to clear her eyes and nose thoroughly before littering it on the road as the car raced through the empty stretch.

"So much for Clean India." Suyash smirked playfully, but Kanika was highly offended yet again by his comment in her emotionally vulnerable state. His words were akin to an arrow that was aimed to pierce her heart.

"Stop the car... stop the car now!" She started bawling while thumping her hands and legs.

"What happened, babe?" Suyash was both amused and surprised at her reaction and hit the brakes again in the less than a minute.

He had not expected her to behave that weirdly until then!

Kanika tried to unlock the door the moment the vehicle came to a halt with a screech! Suyash ensured that she was unsuccessful and caught her.

"What's wrong babe? Just tell me." He asked turning her forcefully towards himself.

"You love Modiji more than me..." Kanika replied while still looking away from him, "I don't want to be with you anymore. You go and stay with him only!"

Suyash had to push his self-control to the breaking point in order to stop himself from bursting out laughing at her reply. He averted his gaze from her and took a deep breath before returning his gaze to hers. "See, you are even laughing." Kanika started crying again.

"*Offo*! I am sorry honey. I just love you..." He said while holding his ears and said in continuance, "You want to drive babe?" The question suddenly grabbed all her attention. She thought she was hallucinating.

"What...?"

"Would you like to drive?"

"You are saying this only because you know that I don't know how to drive a car!" She replied sarcastically.

"Heyy, I am serious! Let us drive it together."

"I don't think that is a good idea." She said as he signalled her to come on his lap.

Kanika continued hollering, "No, no, no!" but had her butt on Suyash's lap and hands on the steering wheel in a jiffy. She had just been pretending to refuse when she never actually tried to resist as he pulled her onto him.

The plush feel of the car plus the alcohol and those two coupled with a carnal touch of the skins in proximity gave wings to the lovers immediately.

Suyash said, "You know about ABC, right?"

"I know I know! Accelerator, Brakes and Clutch. I know all about your car Mr Suyash. I had those in my theory classes when I joined a driving school during my college days. You know my parents could not afford a car so I didn't get a chance to drive much. You know low middle-class people!" Kanika turned emotional by the time she reached the end of her sentence.

"C'mon now babe." Suyash was already fighting through a testosterone upsurge.

"Yeah... Yeah. But I haven't forgotten anything." She chirped the very next moment.

"Wow! So, give me a ride babe.!" His voice turned way smokier.

The two had been staying together for a couple of weeks by then, but they had never been that close physically. It was actually Kanika who had maintained her distance. She wanted to save it until marriage. Suyash had tried to escalate imminence a few times, but she backed out every time. She always felt that things were happening too fast, but that evening was too much to retreat.

Hormonal gushes were already at the peak...!

Vrooooooom! The engines of the Audi raced and she felt enormous vibrations in every part of her body.

The car zoomed through the empty road and even though the steering was with her; the man had full control over everything: The car, the situation and the girl!

Things soon got out of his hands and Kanika started to feel his shaft getting hard under her.

She was going through an emotional roller coaster. She had never been that close to any man and never knew how it would feel and that time when it happened... She wanted it to stop... yet wanted it to continue... She was so confused regarding what she wanted, but she didn't utter a word! She decided to go with the flow and soon realised that she was getting wetter with every passing moment.

On the other hand, Suyash was trying extremely hard to control his emotions. He did not want to ruin anything; he did not want her to think that he was with her for sex; but he wanted to have sex with her and that too not a one timer! He needed much more!

The two sets of eyes in the car were on the road, but all their senses were focussed on each other. Even a subtle movement by any one made them miss a beat. The devastating storm inside them was veiled by a pin drop silence outside!

Things took an abrupt turn when Suyash slipped his fingers inside her dress cursorily. The sensations made Kanika shudder, but she didn't offer any physical resistance whatsoever. The fact was that she had been waiting for it, too!

She, however, said with a big naughty smile, "Hey! What's that? haa?"

Suyash skated in further and she pressed it against herself mechanically. She let go of it instantly as she had no intention to stop him. His fingers flitted further into her bra clumsily and a groan left her lips perfunctorily, "Aaaah...!"

That was the first time in forever that someone else had touched them and she felt amazingly strange. A strong wave of pleasure coupled with insignificant pain initiated from the point of contact and spiralled throughout her body.

The two were cruising in their own world when suddenly there was a big thud and the car came to a halt with a jerk.

"Shit!" They shouted in unison.

The intoxication vanished in less than a microsecond as they had hit something hard. They rushed out to check and heaved a sigh of relief at the sight outside. The merry couple had gone off the road and rammed into the footpath.

Suyash then checked if there had been any damage to the car and realised that lady luck was on their side. They looked at each other mischievously and started laughing outrageously!

The two bodies were on fire by the time they reached their flat. They did not want to wait even a second longer. That was for the first time in her life that Kanika was raring to get rid of her virginity.

They had waited, walked and smiled patiently through the way and an unrelenting pandemonium took reign the moment they stepped into the flat. Suyash behaved like a starved wild animal that had suddenly been uncaged and pounced on her hungrily.

His desperation was damn hot! He pinned her against the wall and kicked the door hard. It closed with a loud bang and she did not give a shit to what happened to the door. All her senses were focussed on one and only one man, Suyash.

She was shivering due to extreme hormonal insurgences and she was trying rigorously to keep herself in control. She however did not know why she wanted to withhold anything? May be because she felt shy or may be her sixth sense wanted to hold her back. But she was in no condition to give a damn to anything else! She was all bent on cruising towards the other side!

Suyash put his index finger on her chin and lifted her face upwards towards him. She looked into his watery eyes that said, “I want you Kanika. I want you now.”

She replied with synonymous ardour, “I am all yours Suyash!”

He reached closer to her after the passionate wordless conversation! His hands on her waist gave her a soulful tingling sensation and the proximity filled her nostrils with the aroma of his cologne. It was only when she had started living with him that she had realised that the smell could actually turn her on, just like they showed in the ads! And this was the time when she was already on the verge of a breakdown! Things seemed ten thousand times sexier to her at that moment.

And then it happened! Their lips touched each other's for the first time and everything around stopped. Their tongues played with one another and her heart pounded heavily as her entire body started feeling wobbly. The two young lovers tore off all the bondages of fear and shyness that evening as they became one!

Love and Squabble

Sex, an act that Kanika had tried her best to abstain from, soon turned synonymous to having a cup of tea! After all, how long can a human protect itself from a blood thirsty vampire with an agenda?

Adding to it, the extremely desirable and highly chiselled body of Suyash that housed a heart that was filled with unending love for Kanika (that's what he made her believe).

Yet again, his mind was a warehouse of unimaginably beautiful and sensual ideas and Kanika walked hand in hand with him through a new and uncharted territory every other day. He did stuff to her and made her do a lot more! She was stunned at his creativity that made her moan and groan and scream before she came vociferously and fall down dog-tired on the bed every single time.

Again, Suyash's body had a lot of bruise marks all over – the aftermath of that ghastly accident that had sent him into a coma, as he told her – was an absolute turn on for her. She loved digging those, but had had goose bumps all over her body one evening when he started describing the wounds and the pain. She stopped him midway!

Kanika was leading a dream life with no clue of the darkness she was heading into!

Leave aside the sex part, the Marketing Head of a leading bank, who should have been extremely busy, had all the time in the world for her! It happened more than once that he left meetings for her. Of course, Kanika would not have allowed that had he told her about even one of them! There were even times when she had to force him to know if he was busy by binding him to promises; and as stupid as it may sound, that worked on him.

All of this made her feel extra special. He gave his girl precedence over everything else, even his work. Kanika never thought that she could do even ten percent of what he did. She felt that she was blessed to have him in her life!

How can a man be so perfect? She used to wonder!

* * *

4 February 2019 (Monday)

However, time started to unfold some really awkward scenarios that added to the foundation of negativity in their relationship! Various small and arguably insignificant changes in Suyash's behaviour began taking a toll on Kanika. The biggest of those was his snappy retorts whenever she touched his phone.

Although, she was not that sneaky girlfriend, who poked her nose into every business of their boyfriends, not giving them space to even breathe, his action seemed unacceptable to her because she would not have had a problem if he used her phone.

Furthermore, she had noticed in the later part of their stay in her flat that Suyash either stepped out of the house or went to a *safe distance* to attend some of his calls. She was offended by it every time, but drank all of it silently as she did not want to make an issue out of it.

We as humans are at times inclined to do things that hurt us; things we don't want to do; things that have been against our personality to avoid a conflict with our loved ones! The only reason that we continue to suffer is our hope, a hope that everything would be sorted out easily. Sometimes it works, most of the time it doesn't! And the latter happened with her.

It was a normal start of the day and Suyash was in the washroom when his mobile rang continuously. Kanika took a sneak peak, just out of curiosity. The screen flashed *Baba.*

She assumed it to be his father and in her quest to impress her father-in-law, she received and said respectfully, "Hello... *Baba. Pao laago...*"

Nobody responded from the other side, but Suyash came out rushing and snatched the phone from her hand and disconnected the call.

"Don't do it... EVER!" He threatened her sternly with a finger pointed towards her face and his gaze fixed straight into her eyes.

Kanika was scared. She had never seen that look in his eyes and started shivering in fear. She didn't know what wrong she had done. Tears rolled down; her mouth still wide open as he turned his back on her, fiddling with his phone.

"What the fuck is your problem Suyash?" Kanika shouted after minutes of silence gathering courage to react. She was utterly shocked at his abrupt behaviour and things had gone way beyond for her to bear.

He looked into her eyes coldly, "Don't take my calls Kanika!"

She retaliated immediately with synonymous insolence, "Don't you dare give me this Suyash and what's your problem, who was it? Was it some whore you have been fucking behind my back? Just fucking tell me?"

"He is my dad." He replied in an irritated voice.

"That's what I thought before your reaction, but now I have differing thoughts."

"You can think whatever you want Kanika," he said and turned away.

"Don't you turn your back on me Suyash. Answer me! What was the problem if I talked to your dad? He already knows that we are staying together, right? As a matter of fact, he thinks that we are married." Kanika yelled at him.

"I don't want to talk about it anymore! Please, it was a mistake."

"So, I am now a mistake?" The words pierced her heart and she yelped in pain.

"Not you! Me telling my parents about our live-in setup, that was a mistake," he said and walked out of the door, leaving a thousand questions lurking in Kanika's mind.

The Oaktree

8 February 2019
(Friday, 6:45 PM)

Nothing remained the same after that day. A qualm had taken birth in Kanika's mind! She could not have denied the chances that he was processing a parallel affair, but she wanted to believe that there was something about his family having issues with the live-in setup. She even tried to talk it out with Suyash with an intent to help, but all her attempts failed. He was adamant to not discuss anything with her!

Kanika, as emotionally and physically invested as she was in him, was getting desperate with every passing moment. She did not want to lose him, but she needed an answer for the behavioural change that was tearing their relationship apart; an answer for that day's action that was extremely uncalled for and an answer whether he wanted to continue with her. Although she was quite unsure of the third part. But, clarity was the need of the hour.

It is said that nature blesses us with whatever we yearn for with all our hearts. The same happened with Kanika as things aligned themselves for her that Friday evening. The two had not been talking much recently and that day had been worse.

The whole day had been boring for Kanika and she did not expect it to get any better on her way to a weekend party with her colleagues. She was lost in her own thoughts, while the car raced towards *Café Modesta* on the Vidhan Sabha Road. Just then, Kanika sighted Suyash's car parked outside one of the restaurants and shouted reflexively, "Please stop the car!"

All the eyes turned towards her questioningly and one of her colleagues, Manisha asked, "What happened Kanika?"

"I see his car there." She pointed towards the black Audi and continued, "I want to surprise him. Then I will join you guys!"

Tulika who was completely unaware of the recent turmoil in Kanika's life said, "Whoooo! Bring *Jijaji* also."

"Yeah sure!" Kanika smiled and hopped out, "See you guys!"

She walked inside *The Oaktree Restaurant* shakily with a zillion apprehensions. Her eyes combed through the thin crowd inside and spotted him sitting with an elderly gentleman with ease.

"Thank god!" She sighed in relief, "He must be some client!"

At least her initial apprehension to find him with another girl was proved wrong and she was never happier to have been incorrect. She wanted everything to be like before at that moment and thought of giving him a call before surprising him with her presence. She wanted every negativity from their relationship to vanish. She was ready to do anything, even if it meant to take the lead and let go of her ego!

She dialled the number and he took the call at the first ring, "Hello..."

That was one thing that she had always admired about him. Even though the things were not working too well between them, he never ignored her calls.

"Hey baby! Where are you?" She said as lovingly as was possible. She was totally in love with him.

"I am in the middle of a meeting," he replied.

"Oh! Sorry to disturb you."

"It's okay!"

"I just wanted you to know one thing," Kanika said with a smile on her face.

"What is it?" She saw his expression change from mild to stern and it made her smile further. She was enjoying it.

"I love you and you are not going to get rid of me that easily babe."

The smile on his face returned as he covered the mouthpiece of his mobile phone and whispered, "I love you too babe and I never want to get rid of you!"

He is so cute... A Marketing Head of a bank, in a meeting with his client, veiling his love talk like a college boy in front of his parent...! She thought with a big smile and asked mechanically, "Where are you now? When will I get to see you?"

"I am in the office. See you at eight!" he said.

She felt a big thud in her heart. All the joy that had piled up in the last few seconds whooshed out noiselessly. She however controlled and asked while looking at him right in front of her, "Oh! So, you are in the office?"

"Yup! Where else would I be?" He continued casually, "I will have to disconnect now. See you in a few hours. Love you!"

"Hmm... Love you too... Bye...!" She said and disconnected the call.

She was stunned and numerous thoughts bombarded her head from all directions. *Why on earth did he lie to me? Who is the man with whom he is sitting? Is it his baba? Is he playing me?* The last thought gave her a mild heart attack and she was inclined to confront him straightaway. But then, she withdrew. Her intelligent side prompted her to take a seat close to them to be able to hear their conversation to get a bit more info. So, she secured a spot soon after by bribing one of the waitresses emotionally and monetarily!

They had been in a conversation for quite some time, but the first thing that Kanika heard the old man speak was, "I think it's already time beta, right?"

"Yes baba. Everything is in place." Suyash replied confidently and then suddenly his voice changed. He turned hateful and continued while grinding his teeth in anger, "This is what they get baba. For everything – I have been a bit tolerant towards the girl only because of you!"

So, then it was confirmed, that was his baba, his dad from that day's call.

What are these two father and son duo cooking together and who the fuck were those people whom he introduced me to because that person was not whom she met on the video chat? Kanika thought confused, *And who would get what for what?*

She had numerous questions in her mind and the only person with the answers were right in front of her eyes. There was no way she could have withheld anymore and reached him in less than a second.

"You liar!" She shouted and slapped him hard before he could have realised her presence. He was shocked as all eyes turned towards her.

"Kanika... you...here... how...?" Suyash stammered.

"Yes... Suyash. I saw your car parked outside and stepped in to surprise you, to make things better for us. But you liar! What the fuck is going on?" She held his collar while shivering in anger and pain.

"Don't create a scene here Kanika." He said holding her wrists, trying to remove her hands from his collars gently.

Kanika, however, did not care about anyone at that time. It was then that he pressed her thumb down, forcing her to draw back painfully.

Suyash then sauntered away from her as Kanika shouted while still trying to absorb the twinge in her thumb, "Where the hell are you going Suyash? Tell me what's going on dammit?"

But, he gave her a deaf ear while talking to the old man, "I will be waiting in the car baba."

"Don't walk out on me, you bastard." She screamed and was about to scuttle behind him when the elderly gentlemen got up and said, "Leave him! I will give you all the answers!"

"Excuse me, who the fuck are you?"

"Mind your language young lady, but of course what more can we expect out of Mr Kunal and Mrs Kriti Chettri's daughter!" Kanika, who was already going after Suyash, stopped immediately at the mention of those name!

"You know my parents?" She was shocked.

"Of course!"

"And you are?"

"I am Suyash's maternal uncle, Rashid Ijaz!"

"And you are his baba, right?" Kanika wanted to confirm.

"Yes, and I am the one who has been taking care of him since his parents died!"

"His parents are dead?"

"Yup."

"Then why the fuck did he lie to me? Why dammit? Everything was a fucking lie!" She yelled in front of everyone in the restaurant and started crying uncontrollably. The staff of the hotel stepped forward to attend to her, but Rashid signalled them to wait.

"Sit down young lady and have some water." Rashid said while filling a glass with some water.

Kanika caught her head and sat down heavily. Everything around her had started spinning. She sipped in some after a few minutes and asked Rashid, "Who were those people over the video chat then?" She was knocked for six at the revelation that had just been made.

"Some paid actors..."

"But why? I need to know why and how the hell do you know my parents?" Kanika was in shock, pain and bewilderment!

"Sit down Kanika. I will tell you a story." Rashid said in a bit shaky but bold voice.

"What story? Do I look like someone in the mood for a story?"

"No... unless you want the answers. *Koi nai...* You can leave if you want to." He shrugged and took the last sip from the mug of coffee placed in front of him.

"Okay old man," She said rudely, "Before any fucking story I need to know a few more things."

"As in...?"

"Is Suyash from Fatehpur?"

"Nope. We are from this very place."

"In that case, should I assume that there was no Manisha or the accident or whatever fucking things he told me about his past."

"Yes."

She was aghast. All that love was a big fucking lie! Her heart broke in to a million pieces instantly!

"But why... why me? What did I do to you guys?" She spoke after a few minutes with utmost difficulty through her absolutely strangulated throat and in the midst of an unstoppable outpour of tears.

"Sins of the past." Rashid replied.

"I fucking never knew Suyash or you. I don't understand a word."

"You will... soon!" He said while passing another tissue towards her.

You cannot be so weak Kanika. A voice inside Kanika's head said, "He cheated on you. You should stop acting like a loser." The word 'loser' suddenly worked magic on her, *I was no fucking loser, a cheater is a loser!* The thought drenched her with courage and fury and she said rigidly, "Okay... Let's hear the explanation you have to defend yourselves!"

Rashid smiled and gestured one of the waiters and asked Kanika, "Would you like to have something?"

"No thanks!"

"Another café Mocha for me and..." He said to the waiter and looked towards Kanika.

"Make that two!" She added and the waiter left as Rashid started speaking, "Things go way back to 2002..."

The Past

Rashid Ijaz tells a story...

6 July 2002
(Saturday, 11:00 PM)

Suyash's eyes opened to a couple of suppressed voices in the house that night. The ten-year-old had dozed off just a few minutes back after wrestling for a long time with his father in his bed. It had become customary for them in the last couple of days to do that every night before cruising towards dreamland! The child recognised one of the voices to be his father's, but was quite unsure of the second male voice. The blanket was pulled up to his face as always, hence Niket didn't know that his son was listening to the conversation.

"Bhaiya, this one last time. Please!" The other voice said and Suyash knew that it was his Bhuvan uncle, Niket's younger brother, whom he had always hated because of the indecorous ways he touched him.

There was a time in the past when Suyash was extremely fond of him. He used to love going out with him and they played almost all the time whenever he was home. They ate together, slept together, bathed together, binge watched serials and movies in their B&W television together and so on.

But it was not very long when Suyash, even at that young age, started feeling something was *not right* about the way Bhuvan always ran his hands inside his clothes.

It was on one of those nights when he was sleeping with his uncle when things went way beyond acceptable for him. The kid was awakened by some weird sensations in the middle of a night. Bhuvan's hands were inside his pants. Suyash was both shocked and frightened and did not know how to react. He just pushed his uncle's hand away and stepped out of the bed.

Bhuvan, who had least expected that, was scared and asked as sweetly as was possible, "What happened *betu*?" His voice had a tremor because he did not want to get in to a situation where he would have to explain his actions to his brother.

"Come back betu." Bhuvan called him again, but the child walked out of the room to sleep with his parents and remained mum about the incident ever after. That was good news for Bhuvan, but there was a drastic change in their relationship after that.

Moreover, the frequency of his visiting them decreased exponentially in the days that followed and Suyash remained at a hand's distance at all times even when he was there. The child was disgusted by him more and more as time flew mainly due to the foul smell of tobacco and pan masala that was Bhuvan's constant accomplice. Suyash was further sickened by the maroon drool he kept on wiping first with his bare hands and then on the sofa cover or the house's curtains all the time. He wished he never visited them.

It had seemed like god had granted his wish, as Bhuvan had not visited them even once in the last one year, but that night was different.

"Shhhh... Keep your voice low. Suyash is sleeping!" Niket hushed Bhuvan.

Why is he here now? Suyash thought, *I hope that he will not stay in our place tonight and even if he does, I hope dad won't let him sleep here with me.* He crossed his fingers and said, "I will move with dad if he comes here."

He was already feeling sick by the repulsive odour released by Bhuvan that entered his nostrils after conquering that thick layer of blanket!

"Okay bhaiya, please... just one last time." He pleaded.

"But why do you need so much money Bhuvan? What happened to all the cash that you got when we sold the southern part of our land last time?" Niket asked him austerely.

"You know it bhaiya. I invested all the money to execute the contract of building a road for a big contractor, but the rain flatlined all my work. The main contractor did not pay me anything and I lost everything for no fault of mine!" He replied.

"Stop all your bullshit excuses Bhuvan! I know you pretty well. You just launder all the money on your drunkard and useless friends. That is not how things work!" Niket had a lot of anger instilled in his voice. He would have definitely shouted had it not have been for Suyash and that hour of the night!

"I am sorry bhaiya. I will do better this time. Please help me. I need this urgently." He pleaded again.

"How much of land do you want to sell this time?"

He replied after a brief pause, "Just twenty thousand square feet..."

"What? Why so much?" Niket was shocked.

"I have plans to open a dhaba on the National Highway. I have even confirmed the location and believe me, it is a fantastic one! Moreover, I have finalised a deal with a very good chef who will bring other workers as per requirement. It is a busy road and we will get lots of customers every day."

He continued after a brief pause, “I have even started communicating with the bus drivers and a few of them have agreed to stop their buses in our place for refreshment every day. I have planned everything thoroughly this time and am not going to ruin anything. I will even get back our land, not only this one, but the previous ones also. Please trust me this last time bhaiya.”

Niket replied, “You say the same thing all the time and the same thing repeats itself all the time.” He continued after a brief pause, “You know this is our ancestral property and I can agree to sell only that much so that I can have something decent left for my son.”

“He is also my son bhaiya. I have now become a responsible person.”

“I know how responsible you are!” Niket replied sarcastically.

He got down on his knees and literally started begging, “Please bhaiya... last time... I promise that I will do whatever you tell me to if I ruin anything this time.”

Niket said, “Okay, I will do it one last time. But remember your promise!”

“Yes bhaiya, here are the papers.” He said and shifted the papers towards Niket and even offered him the pen that he had kept ready in his shirt pocket.

Niket signed the papers quarter-heartedly after giving a good look at them. He did not trust his brother.

“...and have I not told you to not come here after drinking.” Niket said as he returned the papers to Bhuvan.

He replied excitedly while putting the documents inside his bag, “Sorry bhaiya, I took a little because of the tension. Sorry and thanks a lot!”

Niket hummed, “Hmmm...” His voice clearly suggested that he wasn’t happy with what he had done and Suyash started hating his uncle much more from that day. He knew from the conversation that his uncle had forced him to do something he didn't want to. But things were not over. He had to learn more things that night!

Bushra stormed into the room the moment Bhuvan stepped out of the door. She was waiting outside the room eagerly and could wait no more!

"Why did you do it again *ji*?" She said angrily.

"I had to. He is my younger brother; my only family apart from you guys." Niket tried to justify his action.

"I know ji! But this is the fourth time. There is a limit to everything. You know that he has not changed a bit. He is going to squander all that money." Bushra continued after a pause, "He has already sold more than a quarter of our land and continues to fool you every time."

"I know, but..." Niket tried to say something but Bushra interrupted him, "You know there were so many things that we could have provided to our son if you didn't fritter money on him every now and then. Why does our son need to suffer because of your reckless brother?" She had tears in her eyes.

Now that was a shocker for Suyash! Even though quite young, he realised that a lot of his requests had been declined because of his intolerable uncle. The child hated him more from that moment and that dislike was quadrupled because his mother cried because of that man!

"Now leave it no baby!" Niket said lovingly and tried to hug her. She juddered and replied, "Huh... I told you not to entertain him anymore. But who am I to you? Go carry on with your brotherhood. After all, it's your land and money. Who am I to say anything?"

She went out of the room mumbling as Niket switched off the lights and followed her. The later part of the night was spent by Niket trying to cheer up his wife, although unsuccessfully!

That day of bliss

31 December 2002
(Tuesday, 8:00 PM)

It was the New Year's Eve and Mr Niket Krishna, Sales Manager, Amar Finances, had stepped out of the office early that evening to prepare a New Year gift for his son. He couldn't help but smile picturing Suyash's reaction when he would see those colourful and neatly cut flashy tickets to Aqua City, a water park that had started operating in Raipur in the beginning of that year. Niket knew that his son had been ingeminating his intense desire to visit the place for months until then.

Suyash had been pig-headed to step on those extra fascinating rides from the day the local cable TV network provider started floating its advertisement. He was just a kid and those ads are supposed to attract every one of them! Niket had seen how his son's mouth went wide open every time that short twenty second motion picture played. It had almost become a routine for him to say, "Papa, let's go to Aqua City! Please Papa."

"Okay Suyash! We shall go after a few days." This was Niket's routine answer.

"You say this all the time... Please let's go no..." He pleaded all the time, sometimes with folded hands.

"Okay beta! We shall go there next month, after your school tests are over." Niket had to come up with an excuse every time.

How could he tell his child that a big part of his salary went into his education and another part as a saving for his future educational needs because Niket did not want his son to face any financial hindrance to pursue his dreams!

However, Suyash's mind was too gullible to understand that and he usually dozed off, angry at his father. As a matter of fact, the child had started to lose hope of being able to see Aqua City ever in his life. Niket had had it in his mind to fulfil Suyash's desire, but had no idea that his son had been counting the days from the first time he had expressed his interest to his father! It had been seven long months!

However, that day was different. It was going to be a new year, a new month and a new day. A time to start afresh and a time to get rid of old bad memories and what better than to visit the Aqua City?

****

Niket pressed the doorbell and Bushra shouted from the kitchen, "Open the door beta! It must be your dad."

"You go no..." Suyash shouted with his eyes glued to the television set that played his favourite *Tom and Jerry* show.

"Mama is busy no... Open the door betu!" His mom yelled again.

Suyash did not pay attention to what his mom had said until she came right in front of him and shouted balefully, "Suyash... Open the door or I will switch off the television."

That was a chance he was not ready to take. It was better to miss a few seconds rather than the whole episode. The child made a mental analysis of the same and stepped down from his bed reluctantly to take the door. He unbolted while eyes were still stuck on the show and jumped back to his seat in less than five seconds. Suyash was so engrossed that he didn't even take time to look at his father who was standing flashing those tickets in his hands with a big smile. He wanted to exhibit his anger as his mom had forced him to open the door!

Niket was taken aback slightly, but he was a father and knew that all of that came with the bundle. Things may have taken a different turn initially, but he devised a new plan to grab his son's attention immediately to gift him his dream!

He sat down on the sofa that was placed adjacent to Suyash's bed, relaxed and gestured Bushra to sit beside him when she came in with a glass of water. They started a conversation loud enough for Suyash to hear, but soft enough to ensure he did not understand a thing. Their plan failed again as their son was captivated and busy laughing outrageously at the mischief of Jerry!

The couple waited for a few minutes before Bushra spoke loudly in the midst of an ad break, "Leave him, I think he is not at all interested!"

The tone of her voice grabbed all his attention and he started looking towards them as if he had caught them devising a cruel conspiracy against him.

The couple smiled and they blabbered some meaningless stuff softly to get his full attention. Suyash lowered the TV's volume to be able to get a grip on their conversation.

His father was saying to his mother, "Yeah, maybe we should take Archana with us. He will be busy with his Tom and Jerry Show!" (Archana was his class mate and the immediate neighbour.)

"What are they up to?" The words made all of his five senses work at two hundred percent capacity. The name 'Archana' and the words 'taking her somewhere' seemed like a brutal scheme and he asked, "What are you talking about papa?"

"Nothing Suyash. It's just that your papa got some tickets for us to go to Aqua City tomorrow!"

"Wh.... Whaaaaaat...?" Suyash was surprised.

"Yes!" His dad said while showcasing the multi-coloured tickets having miniature pics of various rides and people enjoying them.

"Wow...!" He shouted at the top of his voice and leaped out of the bed immediately.

It was a dream come true for him, so much so that it seemed too good to be real!

"But..." His mother said while keeping those *too good to be real stuff* out of his reach, "We called you so many times, but you seemed highly uninterested so we have now decided to take Archana with us instead of you."

The child felt a thud in his heart and big drops of tears raced through his cheeks within a nano-second! He started crying and shouted, "Nooooooo...!"

He cursed himself for not paying attention to their words and snivelled loudly. Moreover, the talk about Archana joining them pinched him hard!

"*Alle... Mera babu shona.*" His mother said lovingly after a few seconds, "Don't cry." She embraced him with a smile on her lips.

"You won't leave me no?" Suyash said while still sobbing in her lap.

"No sweetheart, we aren't going anywhere without you!" She said while caressing his hair. He was relaxed by her words but he needed to be sure.

"And what about Archana? Don't take her anywhere with you. You won't take her no?" He asked wiping his eyes and nose from the edge of her sari.

"She is not coming with us. I brought tickets only for us son!" Niket replied and showcased the three tickets in his hand. His words made those inexplicable quantities of tears in his eyes vanish faster than they had appeared and drew a big smile on his lips. He jumped on him in excitement and shouted, "Yessssssss...."

He loved to do that. All the time Niket was a strong man and had never allowed him to fall. How would he? His son was his life!

Moreover, Niket was a fitness freak!

Suyash loved to hang on his neck and shoulder like a monkey as his father pulled himself up using the iron rings that he had hung on the mango tree in their garden. He enjoyed the company of his father more than anything else early every morning!

He never left his side and replicated his actions as Niket performed other high-intensity strength workouts! His father even taught him a few moves that he absorbed effortlessly. It was in his blood!

"It's your new year present betu!" Niket said and the child kissed him in excitement.

"Thank you... thank you... thank you... thank you so much papa!" He shouted and hugged him with all his strength, "I love you... Love you."

"*Arey*! All the love only for papa?" His mom interrupted.

He pushed himself closer to his dad and continued hugging him, "Yes!"

Niket gestured his wife to come closer and he hugged her. It was bliss! A perfect family that exhibited the purest form of love! Suyash was in the middle of two people who loved him more than anything else. He was their world and they were his and the child had already started dreaming about the day to come. He was no more interested in crackers or New Year special sweets prepared by his mom. Only one thing hovered in front of eyes – Aqua City!

Pinch me mom!

01 January 2003
(Wednesday, 11:45 AM)

Suyash's mouth went wide open the moment he reached the amusement park.

"Pinch me mom!" He asked his mom, who looked at her son with an 'I know what you mean' smile.

"I just want to be sure that it's not a dream." He chuckled.

His parents smiled at one another and Bushra pinched his arm lightly.

"Ouch! It's real!" He tittered again.

"Shut up, *dramebaaz*!" She said and pulled his cheeks.

Suyash paid no more attention to the conversation between his parents. His gaze was fixed on the gigantic bright yellow board that read *AQUA CITY* in big, bold, beguiling letters. It was penned over a charming image of a blue pond surrounded by rocks in the shades of grey. Big elephant grasses and colourful flowers were drawn peeping through the crevices along with a couple of coconut trees. A number of green coloured frogs – one of it in mid-air while the other diving in to the water – stared right in to Suyash's eyes. Colourful fishes and a few other aquatic animals were showcased frolicking merrily in the water!

He stared at the gigantic rides visible from the outside.

The fact was that they were visible from miles away when

they looked like small toys, but then they had started giving him goosebumps already.

* * * *

12:00 Noon (Aqua City)

"Mom, he looks so much like Popeye!" Suyash exclaimed as they reached the tall gatekeeper dressed in a grey uniform.

"Shhh... He will kick us out if he hears." His mom hushed him trying hard to control her laughter. She, however, realized immediately that her son was right. His face had a strong resemblance to *Popeye the sailor man*: one of Suyash's favourite cartoon characters apart from *Tom and Jerry*.

They then waited in queue for a few minutes until a short lady clad in blue checked the tickets again and placed a blue band on their forearms after receiving it from the man behind the counter. "Don't tear it off or lose it Suyash, else they will force us out!" Niket cautioned his son as they crossed through a maze of metallic pipes to step in to its premises.

Suyash made a mental note to be extra cautious as they walked towards the hanging room to get the clothes provided by the management. They had arrived early, which gave them the opportunity to select the best alternative for themselves. The options were set to decline exponentially as more and more people would pour in.

"Ouch!" Suyash shouted and held on to his dad's shoulder as he was about to fall on that slippery floor. Niket was helping him get into one of those oversized shorts that was the smallest of all the available options!

"It won't slip no, papa?" He asked apprehensively.

Niket tied it tight and put an extra knot, "Don't worry son; it won't fall now!"

"Okay!" His dad's approval filled him with confidence and a big smile clenched his face.

"I look like a rapper, no?" He said while looking at his father.

"Yo!" He said while crossing his hands like rappers and his father joined him instantly.

The duo then paced towards the pool to get wet on New Year's Day on which the outside temperature was hovering around a comfortable 24 degrees Celsius.

Everything including nature was on their side, until then!

Bushra joined her husband and son after a few minutes and they had a gala time in the pool playing with water, splashing it on each other, jumping and playing volleyball. That really was the best day of their lives!

05:00 PM

Suyash gobbled his all-time favourite chicken noodles, chicken chilli and a bottle of soft drink hungrily. He had a hundred rounds of various rides and slides, pool jumps, boat rides and running hither and tither exhausted by then and needed to make up for all those calorific losses immediately.

All that Suyash experienced that day was super butterfly kicks in the gut, inexplicable thrill and full-on *masti!*

The three souls in love were busy celebrating the paramount moment; however, none of them knew that the end was right around the corner! Who does?

Drunken driver

01 January 2003
(Wednesday, 08:30 PM)

That had been the best day of Suyash's life and they reached back home at around eight in the evening. They got their dinner packed from a famous dhaba, situated a kilometre away from their dwelling! It meant the family was free to spend more time with their neighbours.

Archana, Rashi, Amit, Mithun and Suyash tagged along with their dads to burst crackers!

However, Suyash and Mithun were particularly interested in big bloodcurdling bombs that would give a big thump in their chests and draw everyone's attention. They wanted to be the loudest and for the same reason, they had to walk to a spot that was a few metres away from others to plant their favourite fireworks. Moreover, the drama queens in the group, especially Archana, seemed overly frightened and wanted them to shift away further.

Suyash walked a few more steps away to burst one of the biggest bombs that they called *Bada Alu Bomb*, as it looked like a big sized potato.

"*Aur dur ja Suyash* (Go away further, Suyash)!" Archana and Rashi shouted in unison.

He took a few more steps, turned around and asked them, "*Ab thik hai* (Is it okay now)?"

"*Nai nai*... Go away further!" Archana shouted. But Suyash ignored her as that spot seemed perfect for the bomb and his calculation suggested that the explosive was sufficiently and safely distanced from them! So, the girls covered their ears and closed their eyes tightly even before the cracker was lit up!

Suyash smiled proudly and placed his prized possession, the symbol of his courage, on the ground. He was about to light it up when someone caught him from behind and before anything else could happen his body was flung away forcefully.

A huge noise crammed the surrounding, *Boooom!* and then Suyash carped in pain, "Aaaaah...!" as he hit the ground with a big thud.

Everything turned absolutely silent and still for the child for the next few seconds, and all he could remember was seeing his father's face.

It was Niket who had thrown him away. But why? He had no idea.

"Suyash beta, are you okay? Get up beta." The staggered child opened his eyes in the same spot after hearing mysterious voices!

Malhotra dadu and dadi, the old couple living a few houses away, continually tapped his cheek and rubbed his head to wake him up. He had passed out for a few seconds and they were relieved to see the kid wake up. Suyash had lost track of all the preceding events. All he could realize was that his eyes were heavy and he felt very sleepy.

The child was still contemplating the things that had transpired a moment ago. His memory failed. He suffered from amnesia and suddenly, everything crashed down on him like a landslide.

He shouted appallingly, "Where is papa? I saw him throwing me away. Papa... Papa..." and he started looking hither and tither.

His eyes got stuck to a spot. It was the same spot where he had chosen to place his bomb and the same place where his father had reached him out of nowhere and thrown him away and it was the same spot that had become home to a lot of crowd and commotion.

He looked at the Malhotras and shouted, "What happened dadu? Where is mom? Where is dad?"

Mr Malhotra replied, "They are..."

The child ran towards the crowd without heeding anything he said. He was super anxious at the thought of the worst. Dadu tried to stop him, but was neither strong nor fast enough for the child.

He reached the spot and heaved a sigh of relief! His mom and dad were sitting there. They, too, were trying to shake off the fluff in their heads. Suyash ran to his mother, hugged her tight and started crying immediately!

She caressed his hair and asked, "You okay son?"

The child said nothing and continued crying. She pulled him closer to her bosom. Tears were rolling down her cheeks! She had nearly lost her son that evening. It was only because of her husband who saw the waywardly driven car from a distance and ran at lightning speed to reach his son. He had to pick and throw him away to put him out of harm's way; even in that scenario, he had ensured that his son landed on the soft grassy land near Malhotra's house!

Niket had prepared himself mentally and physically in less than a micro second to be run over fatally by the hustling wagon! He was not thinking about himself at that moment; all that mattered then was his son's safety, even at the cost of his life; that is a father's love for his son! The driver, however, managed to spin the steering wheel in that last second just to graze his body marginally before hitting the electric pole.

Niket had beaten death that evening, both his son's and his own. May be that was his destiny! But who knows what destiny wants? The bitter truth is that destiny gets what it wants and they were still to realize that!

In those few seconds, Bushra had followed her husband to save her family. Even she wasn't thinking about herself at that moment. All she could see was the speeding car that was being driven off the road by a careless driver, her son, who seemed to be in the perfect spot to be hit hard by it and her husband, who was sprinting to save him, ready to give up his life and then she got partially struck by it just before it hit the pole!

A young couple, who seemed completely unaffected by the incident, stepped out of the car, babbling among themselves, after a few seconds. The sway in their body and the slur in their voices clearly revealed that they were drunk.

"Bushra, take Suyash inside. I need to teach these people a lesson." Niket said while signalling her wife.

The people continued hollering, "Call the police!"

"The fuckers are drunk."

"Let's beat the hell out of them." and so on.

"Why do you ass holes leave your kids on the road?" The man said trying hard to maintain his balance. It seemed he had no idea of what was going on.

"Leave it honey, these people just know how to make kids and throw them on the road like worms. They don't fucking care about them!" The lady's voice suggested she was tanked!

"What the fuck do you mean?" The already infuriated Niket punched the man right across the face.

The person fell down and started bleeding immediately.

"You mother fucker!" The lady said and slapped him right there and then it was Bushra, who had decided to stay there, jumped in and replied with three to four slaps, making the girl fall down.

"You bastard, how dare you to touch my husband?!" The vexed lady kicked her furiously until Niket held her back.

The man was on his feet by then and shouted, "How dare you hit us? You bunch of swines; all giving birth to insects. Who is going to compensate for this car? All you mother fuckers!"

The crowd lost their cool and started hitting the drunk couple immediately. They were fortunate because the police patrol party crossed that way and took control of the situation.

Then, one of the policemen peeked into the rear seats and shouted, "There is someone else also." and opened the door.

There was an unconscious girl, whose hands and legs were tied and her mouth taped.

"Who is this girl?" The senior police officer asked them.

They stayed mum and the whole crowd was shocked at the revelation.

"They will say everything in the lock-up." He roared and ordered for them to be taken to the police station.

Some people, including Niket, who had cameras, captured their pics and a group FIR was lodged against the driver. They were taken to the police station. At the same time, the unconscious girl was immediately sent to the local hospital!

The entire celebration was doomed because of those reckless criminals. Niket and Bushra thanked the almighty a zillion times and the family resumed their normal life the very next day. Though nothing had stabilised until then, neither their mind nor their body!

Muggers

2 January 2003
(1:30 AM)

"Hey, somebody is knocking on our door." Bushra woke her husband, who was dead asleep.

"There is nobody. You must be dreaming!" He said in his deep slumber and started snoozing immediately.

"C'mon get up, someone is definitely there." Bushra nudged her husband hard to get him out of his sleep.

Khat khat khat! That time even he heard that.

"Uff..." He checked his watch using his pencil torch and said, "It's 1:30."

"Yes! But who has come at this hour?" He said and got out of bed to switch on the lights.

"Maybe it's an emergency, but in that case, people outside could have called us," Bushra said thoughtfully.

"In that case, only one person would come and knock our door now." He grumbled and went out to take the door.

"You and your brother. I understand nothing." Bushra said irritated.

Niket switched on the drawing room lights where Suyash was busy playing with angels in his dream and asked softly, "Who's there?"

"It's Bhuvan!" The voice from outside said. He was right!

He recognized him immediately and opened the door, "Is it any time to come Bhuvan!" He said irritated.

"Sorry bhaiya. But it was damn urgent. It couldn't have waited until morning." He said while stepping inside.

"Shhh... Suyash is sleeping. Keep your voice low."

"Sorry!" Bhuvan replied.

"So, what is the urgency?"

"Actually..." Six masked people with a bag rushed into the house as Bhuvan continued, "I owe these people some money and they are not ready to wait."

"Who are these people?" Niket tried to keep his voice low. He sensed the danger and his mind started working overtime. He was a fighter, but a wrong move would jeopardize his family's safety. Moreover, six was too much for anyone. So, he started thinking hard, went near Bhuvan, and whispered, "Why did you bring them here?"

"I had no option bhaiya."

He then turned towards them and said, "I don't know what he owes you. But I am a family man and this is a bad time for me. So I promise to take care of whatever this asshole owes you tomorrow!"

"Now!" One of them roared.

His voice was strong enough to take Suyash out of his dreams and pull Bushra out of bed.

"Please keep your voice low. My kid will be frightened if he gets up and he sees all of you." Niket pleaded with folded hands.

"Hmmm..." One of them groaned with a voice still at the fifth level.

"How much does he owe you?" Niket asked.

"Much more than you can give right now." The same masked person said.

"Don't worry. I will clear everything tomorrow, please leave now." Niket's hands were still folded.

Just then Bushra entered the room hearing the commotion and exclaimed, "Who are these people?"

Niket turned towards his wife and said, "You go inside. I will take care of them!" And suddenly there was a big thud *Baam!* One of the men hit Suyash's father with a rod from behind and he dropped unconscious over Bushra's face right away!

"Noooo!" The flabbergasted woman shouted looking at her husband's blood that poured out uncontrollably.

Just then, one of them hauled the sleeping child and put a big knife around his neck and said, "You make a sound and you will see his dead face."

"Please don't!" Bushra begged while putting her comatose husband on the floor. Bhuvan was standing right there with a big smile and walked out of the house uncaringly the moment her helpless sister-in-law looked at him with pleading and tear-filled eyes.

Suyash was shocked as the jerk put him out of his sleep. He saw his father bleeding on the ground and his mother snivelling outrageously while trying to stop the bleeding. He was hooked up to a pair of rough hands that seemed to squeeze the life out of him and a big knife flashed around his neck.

That was more than enough to scare the shit out of him and he started bawling uncontrollably while wriggling to get out of that man's grip. The man with the knife, grasped him harder and shoved his hand onto his mouth and nose, making it literally impossible for the child to even breathe.

Suyash turned asphyxiated within seconds when one of them said, "If you cry son, or hit him, we will kill you and your mother."

"Please stop. He is just a child!" Bushra shouted and got up to get her hands on her son.

"Don't you dare take another step or!" The man who seemed like the leader said gesturing 'slashing the throat'.

"Okay okay... No no." She stopped immediately and then looked towards her son and said, "Don't cry Suyash. You are a strong boy."

The man slowly emancipated the grip to ensure that the child didn't die right then. A lot had to be done before he breathed his last. Suyash however continued sobbing helplessly as his mom said, "All will be good Suyash. You are a brave boy. Just like your dad!"

"Yes Suyash, you are brave." One of them mocked and the monsters started guffawing.

"What the fuck do you people want?" Bushra cried outrageously looking at Niket who was bleeding profusely, both from his skull and one of his ears.

Two of the freaks removed their masks in response and Bushra was stunned to see the faces.

"You? How? You should be in jail?" She went berserk and hollered.

They were the drunken couple from the other night, who had been arrested and locked up by the cops. She was confused, tried to connect the dots and strived to establish the type of association they had with Bhuvan. Nothing clicked!

The boss woman then looked at her husband and said with a wicked smile, "See, I told you. She would be shaken and we would enjoy!"

"Yes, honey." The man raised his hands and replied, "You were right when you said that their reaction would be absolutely adorable when they see us." He paused momentarily and said, "But it is really such a shame that our big hero is kind of out of his senses.' Saying so, he kicked the legs of the defencelessly lying Niket.

"Just stop it." Bushra implored, trying to protect her husband from those kicks and asked, "What do you want?"

The lady said, "If you want your son and husband alive, you will do exactly what we tell you to?"

Bushra was highly apprehensive and her heart throbbed at the uncertain. But Niket and Suyash were dearer to her than her life and she was ready to do anything to save them. She knew she had no option, but to do as told. She replied, "I am listening."

The couple looked at each other and the lady said with a sly smile, "Let's go to your bedroom."

"Wh...Why...?" Her eyes went wide open. That was the last thing she had expected.

"You can waste time with your stupid questions or we can go inside!" The lady replied.

"Okay... We will..." Bushra replied submissively and continued with folded hands, "But can someone please take him to the hospital. He will die!"

"Nobody is stepping out before you give us what we need. So, if you want to save your husband, I suggest you do whatever we say, quickly!" The hard-hearted lady replied cunningly.

"Hmm... Come inside." Bushra said to the lady who caught hold of her husband (or boyfriend) and went in hurriedly. She wanted to finish everything quickly so that she can take her dying husband to the hospital. However, three other men followed them inside uninvited, while one of them stayed out with the child and the half-dead Niket!

Things that happened within the four walls

The lady took out a big video camera from the bag and said, "Remove your clothes! One by one... Slowly!"

"What?" Bushra was shocked at her words, "You want me to undress in front of all these men and this camera?"

"Yes! Did I speak Latin or French or any other language that you don't understand?" The lady said knitting her eyebrows together.

"Sorry, that's not happening." Bushra replied sternly.

"It's going to happen. If you want to save your family?" She said with a wicked smile.

"Please, don't make me do this!" Bushra burst into tears immediately. She went down on her knees with folded hands, pleading continuously, "Please, I beg of you."

"You should have thought of all that before hitting and filing an FIR against us!"

"I am sorry, please forgive us." Bushra started rubbing her forehead on the woman's feet.

The lady kicked her on the shoulder, pushing her away and said, "Enough of all this drama. Just remove your fucking clothes."

She continued crying and imploring mercy when her husband (or boyfriend) said, "Uff! Let's just kill them and leave."

Bushra was stunned. She wasn't worried about her life, but there was no way she was going to put her family at risk. She got up immediately and said, "No, no... I will do it..."

"Great, let's not waste more time than we already have." The lady said with a sinister smile.

Bushra felt extremely helpless. She had no choice. Her neighbours would take more than just a few minutes to get out of their sleep and respond if she shouted. But that would give them sufficient time to kill everyone and leave and there was no way she could have let that happen.

***

Tears rolled down continuously as she prepared herself for the embarrassment and humiliation that was ready to destroy her! The act that she was forced to perform had not even occurred in her wildest of dreams. Every part of her body had been veiled since her childhood days.

One last time she looked straight into her eyes and said softly, "Please don't make me do this... please... please... please... You are a woman. Please understand."

The lady said, "Uff! Even you made us spend time in jail. If we kidnapped and drugged a girl for our business, why did you have to interfere?"

The man joined in and continued, "... And now because of you and your husband, our names are in the police record and we cannot continue here any longer. We just had to make videos of that girl and then we could make good money, but now that you people have spoilt that, it is you who is going compensate for our losses and sponsor our business in a new place."

"... And you look pretty good." The lady said, touching her lips and cheeks.

Bushra shuddered and looked away in disgust.

"C'mon now, don't waste more time. You remember, your husband and your son...?" The man said with fake concern, "We don't want to finish off your happy family."

The words put Bushra into quick action mode and she started removing her clothes, starting from her kurti, one by one!

"That's like a good girl. You look absolutely amazing!" The lady said joyfully, "It's not going to take much time."

In the next few minutes, Bushra stood in front of five sighing strangers (four men and a woman), a camera and her absolutely ruined self-image, completely naked.

"Wow! You are still so hot. See I told you." The woman said as the group high-fived each other.

Bushra saw the three men salivating like street dogs and pleaded looking at the lady, "You got what you wanted. Can I please put back my clothes?"

"Not now! You have to do a few stuff." The Nepali lady beamed impishly.

"What stuff?" She was alarmed. The assumption of their intention made her shiver in fear.

"You need to suck this man!" She said and pushed one of the men right in front of her.

"No... no...no... no... please no. I haven't touched any man except Niket, even in my dreams... please don't." Bushra begged earnestly as the unfeeling monsters laughed continuously.

"Variety is the spice of life honey, and I am damn sure this person's tool is better than your husband's." She said while signalling that man to undress.

"Please don't make me do this."

"Uff! Your husband's life expectancy will decrease with your delay!" The man beside her said once again, "We want you all to live happily ever after."

The lady continued and said to Bushra devilishly, "You can leave the moment he finishes."

Bushra sat on her knees as the person dropped his pants right in front of her face and initiated the act. She was giving her best to get over with everything quickly when another caught her from behind and started fiddling with her body.

"Please stop!" Bushra cried.

"Nobody's going to stop. I am getting a perfect video. I think three-some will be a good idea." The witch announced, enjoying every bit of it.

"Nope. Make it foursome." The lady's husband said and signalled the last remaining man to join.

"Yes, perfect." The third person jumped in immediately and they gnawed her like an animal until all of them ejaculated all over her.

Bushra was in tremendous agony, but she did not shout or make a sound. She suffered all of that pain voicelessly to save her child and her husband. Moreover, she did not want her son, who was wide awake in the other room to get a clue of whatever was happening to her inside. So, she lay on her bed motionless for the minutes that followed after being maltreated viciously.

"Thanks a lot madam. Now you can go wherever you want to go!" The lady said while putting the camera back into the bag and all of them left soon after!

Bushra gathered all the strength that was left in her and got into her clothes. She was suffering from intense vaginal and anal bleeding. Her legs were shaky and she fell down the moment she tried to walk out of the room.

But she had to get up. She had to take her dying husband to the hospital, but she felt helpless! And then she put together everything that was left in her and started shouting at the top of her voice, "Help... help... Somebody!"

The person outside had thrown Suyash against the wall before leaving. The impact had rendered the child unconscious.

The shouts woke up a lot of neighbours, but nobody was able to reach the angst-ridden family in time. Those bastards had latched the doors of all the neighbours from outside before knocking Niket's door to ensure their safe escape at any point of time. Someone called another person from a different neighbourhood for help. They reached, but only after everything was finished!

Into the trap

Suyash was left all alone in this whole wide world. All he had was his hateful uncle Bhuvan staying with him in that house. The child yearned for someone else, his Rashid Mama, but he was nowhere to be seen. He had met him last on the thirtieth of December, after which he had gone away on a long holiday with his friends. The child however, at that time, wanted nothing else but him. Then again, destiny had already made a setup for him to suffer more and for that it was necessary that Rashid was away!

Everyone around, including Suyash were completely ignorant of Bhuvan's direct involvement in the catastrophe that had turned a happy family to dust! He had successfully dodged everyone that night and had come back to the same home he had wreaked havoc as a bereaved brother in tears!

One should have watched him cry that day. He would have shamed professional mourners!

The way he did that and the way he showcased love and care for Suyash could have easily fetched him an Oscar for his performance that day!

Everyone (including the child) was so convinced by his actions in the next few days that they agreed for him to take up the responsibility of the child from that day on!

Suyash had started to treat him as a father figure in just a couple of days! That is how a human mind works. We tend to grasp even a straw while drowning and there he got a full-grown man, his own uncle, who seemed to have transformed completely after his big brothers' death!

The child even agreed, although reluctantly, to shift to his uncle's place; i.e., the village that was more than a hundred kilometres from the city of Raipur.

That was the village where Niket and Bhuvan's great-great grandfathers used to live and cultivate. They had a big agricultural land there and he promised everyone that he would ensure that his nephew would get admitted to a school nearby. He also promised to take good care of him and everybody including Suyash was already in his trap!

Dirt, damp, pain and stain

18 February 2003
(Tuesday, 9:30 PM)

Things had turned around massively for Suyash after that horrendous night. He lost the freedom of choice. It didn't matter whom he hated or loved or what he wanted or not! He had to bow down before destiny, and worse, he understood that at a very young age!

Bhuvan, who had masked himself with fake love and concern, had started portraying his real self in seclusion. He didn't care if the child ate or slept or even died. Things got more grim with every passing day. Suyash yearned for love; he needed care and attention; he however had no idea of the loathsome episode that was about to splatter him into pieces!

***

He had dozed off early that evening after having his dinner and was playing with his dad in his dreams. The smile said it all!

Khat khat khat!

The loud knock cruelly took him out of his peaceful sleep.

"Get up you bastard! Are you dead?" Bhuvan shouted impatiently.

The terrifying voice made the child, swirling in siesta, fly at lightning speed to unbolt the door.

"Were you fucking yourself?" He roared stepping in.

"N...N...No... Sorry, uncle." Suyash replied, trying hard to regain his composure and not to cry.

"I will rip your tongue and hang you there if you make me wait the next time." He said while pointing towards a hook that was hung on one of the logs in the ceiling.

The terrified child swallowed a big lump in his throat while imagining himself lynched and wiping the beads of sweat on his temple.

He sighed in relief as Bhuvan walked towards the kitchen in his blue chequered lungi and the dirty white vest that hadn't been washed in days, to get something to eat. He was a dark and hefty man; at least six feet in height and a waist circumference that ensured he wouldn't be able to see his toes ever.

Suyash watched him lick his fingers after finishing the entire plate of rice, dal and brinjal curry within five minutes. His heart beat increased sporadically each time he licked one of his fingers and winked at him. He was frightened; damn frightened. Although nothing terrible had happened to the child till that night (except for uncalled scolding throughout the day, a few slaps as and when Bhuvan wanted for no reason at all and filthy slang while drinking in front of Suyash), a fear of something unknown gripped him that night! He started shivering like a dry leaf.

"Did you eat nicely beta?" Bhuvan asked with fake concern while caressing his hair.

"Yes." Suyash answered softly. He cringed as he did not like his touch, ever!

"Oh... *mera* beta... I love you." He said with a lot of lust topped with evil in his voice, nearing him.

"Leave me uncle! What are you doing?" Suyash shouted the moment Bhuvan caught him and put his hand inside the striped half-torn t-shirt of the child and removed it instantly.

Suyash knew very well that his uncle had no intention of making him bathe at that hour of the evening. Bhuvan was the most unhygienic person known to him and he was drunk. The ten-year-old kid ran towards the door, but he was not tall enough to reach the latch on the upper side of the door. He was stuck within the four walls of the house with the most unwanted person in the world. He started crying vehemently as his uncle stepped towards him.

Suyash banged the door until his hands and leg started hurting badly. He shouted for help at the top of his voice, but nobody came. The fact was that there was nobody around. He was in his uncle's house, that was situated in the middle of the fields, isolated from all other dwellings of the vicinity. There was no way that the child's voice could have reached any of the ears that far!

His uncle, Mr Bhuvan Krishna, owned a big land which he had inherited from his forefathers, and now that Suyash's dad was dead, he was the sole owner of everything; the reason why he helped those people kill his own brother!

He wasn't employed and was too lazy to work in the fields. Above all, he was an alcoholic. That too, not an ordinary one, but the kind who could shame the pigs after getting drunk.

Suyash was terrified to the core. His legs gave up due to the shivering and he fell down. He continued yelling at the top of his voice, but his strength soon started giving up on him. His uncle realised that and neared him with an evil smile.

He caught him by his arms and pulled his old navy-blue half pant in one big jerky movement. That pant was the only memory of him being a student of St. Margaret School, when his parents were alive!

Suyash was quite unaware of his intentions until then. He didn't know why he was stripped nude. What he did understand very well was that he had to save himself and did the only thing that seemed best – he bit Bhuvan's hand as hard as he could.

"*Aaaaahhh...*" Bhuvan groaned in pain and let go of him immediately.

He turned red in anger as he saw drops of blood on his forearm. Suyash had actually gnawed through his rough skin and made him bleed!

"Just wait now, you asshole. You dare to bite me like this." He shouted angrily and pounced towards the naked child in rage.

Suyash had ran to the farthest corner of the room and sat on the floor while trying to cover his private parts using his limbs. He was frightened to the soul, he was ashamed to the zenith, he felt awfully vulnerable and he missed his mom and dad.

The child shouted, "Ma... Papa..." as his uncle caught him by his neck while pushing his body against the wall to make him immobile.

Baaam... Baaam... Baaam... Baaaam... He gave the poor child blows after blows all across his small naked body that turned red and then blue within moments.

Suyash continued yelling in pain as Bhuvan dragged him through the room and brought him to the veranda near the grill and threw him there. The child rubbed his entire body trying to relieve himself of the immense pain he felt, while crying continually as his uncle stepped away. He was in great pain, but the thought that things were done for the night gave him some respite. However, he was hell wrong!

He heard Bhuvan's footsteps nearing him once again and his blubbers intensified the moment he saw those red fiery eyes. He had a rope and a couple of rough fire sticks in his hands! Suyash wanted to get up and run, but he froze like dead making things handsomely easy for him. Bhuvan seized the already helpless child to ensure zero resistance and then the big fat man half sat on his tiny body while tying his hands and legs to the grill.

Suyash was horrified and peed right there in his fear!

How he missed his parents! How he hated god!

The so-called man then showed him his hand and shouted, "You are going to bite me like this, you bastard?"

"No....N... N.... Na....." The child mumbled, finding it difficult to breathe as he saw the toothed weapon ready to tear him.

Baaam... baaam... baaaam... He hit him thrice as Suyash yelled in pain and shouted, "I am sorry uncle. I will not do it ever again. I am sorry!"

He laughed, "Your sorry isn't good enough." and hit him again. *Baaam... baaam... baaam...*

"Aaaaah.... Aaaaah..." The child continued yelping as his skin opened up in multiple spots and started bleeding.

He then threw the stick away and shouted, "Now stay here the whole night." He went inside and bolted the door.

Suyash's vociferous sobs transformed into whimpers in the next few minutes as he realized that the foul-mouthed spiteful monster was gone. However, the tears had decided to continue erupting disobediently in his intense agony as he reiterated just two words over and over and over, "Ma... Papa..."

His voice got lower with time as he fell asleep on cold concrete, damp and stained by his own piss! The child's bruised and tired body gave in to the much-needed sleep.

Ripped apart

The night of grief was not yet over for the child!

"Aaaah..." Suyash muttered with closed eyes. He felt a touch on one of his bruises and the throbbing brought him back to the real world; a world of pain!

His eyes went wide to see his uncle right in front of him in the middle of the night. He tried to run away in horror. However, he failed massively as his hands and legs were still tied to the sturdy iron grills and there was no way for him to go anywhere.

He started yelling at the top of his voice at the conjecture of multiplied laceration when Bhuvan said, "I am so sorry beta, but you enraged me so badly."

His words were accompanied by his hands constantly moving all around his body. Suyash looked away in fear, disgust and anguish.

"You know your uncle loves you very much, no?"

Suyash remained mum, trying hard to keep his tears at bay.

"...and you know what your uncle just wants you to love him back as he does to you." He said with an evil smile.

The innocent child had no idea what the monster meant and kept looking away in to the darkness, clueless of the agony that was going to haunt him for a lifetime!

Love – the small four-letter word meant whatever he had experienced with his parents, and no matter how young he might have been, he knew that Bhuvan was nowhere close to loving him!

The child was shaken and started crying again, "Please leave me uncle. Please... Please... I won't do it again."

The innocent soul thought that all of those were his punishment as he had bit him hard. He had no idea that his uncle had all the intention to do it ever since he had stepped into the house that evening or may be even before. Who knew?

The child continued yelling and crying, "Please leave me uncle... please. I beg of you... please!"

"You are not going to understand the easy way!" Bhuvan shouted and sprinted inside.

Suyash saw his naked uncle get out of his sight and started crying louder at the supposition of excruciating pain that was about to follow!

He wasn't wrong. His uncle came back with the same rough and spiky sticks that had been used on him mercilessly a few hours ago!

He was appalled and started yelling at the top of his voice, "I am sorry... sorry... please leave me. I will do whatever you tell me... Don't hit me please." He had endured enough pain that evening and was in no condition to take any more of that beating that took out skins each time they touched him.

What would be worse? He thought and opened his mouth immediately.

"See... *laaton ke bhoot baton se nai maante...* Stubborn children like you do not understand the soft language of love!" His uncle jeered and started fidgeting with his phallus in front of his eyes.

The child again saw something he wasn't supposed to see. He witnessed the shaft getting bigger and harder. And then once again his uncle was uncomfortably close to him and filth filled his senses yet again!

"C'mon kid, you are going to enjoy this as much as I would. I am sure you wouldn't have gotten this pleasure if you were with your parents." A malevolent smile had etched itself from his left to right ear as he got closer.

The child made his best effort to obey while trying to control his tears when his uncle hollered, "Open it up, don't make me wait any longer." He spoke while twiddling it intensely.

His uncle thrust that stinky thing into his mouth.

He was choked immediately; he wanted to shout, but his voice was clogged by the thing that had crammed every corner of his mouth up to his throat.

Aa... aa... mm... mmmm... Were the only sounds that left his tender voice box.

His hands and legs were tied and his head was pinned against the iron grill behind him. Oxygen had been cut off from his body and he saw darkness in front of his eyes. He wriggled while his uncle continued thrusting his shaft into his mouth as Suyash squirmed intensely for a single breath!

The child was about to give up on life when Bhuvan groaned loudly, "Aaaaaaaaaagh..." and released the white semi-dense sticky fluid inside his mouth and all over his face and body and came out of him while still fidgeting and releasing all the leftovers on him.

The child lost consciousness for the following few seconds and puked out everything that he had eaten that evening right there the moment he regained his senses. He had no idea that he had just been fucked by his uncle, but he was disgusted to the soul! He wiped his mouth on the iron grill behind him while spitting out all of that repulsive emission that had stirred his stomach.

"You are free now betu!" Bhuvan said and opened his hands and legs.

He ran staggeringly towards the bathroom, switched on the tap and rinsed his mouth the hundredth time before sitting under it and crying ferociously. He cleaned his tongue, again and again with the stainless-steel tongue cleaner until he scraped out the skin and spat blood! He wanted to get rid of everything that seemed to have become a part of the cells in the mouth. However, nothing changed and he vomited again! The stench had latched itself to his breath and his body.

The water flowed all through his body, making him feel no better. He rubbed the soap all over his body, but nothing changed. He did it again and again, but everything seemed useless.

He wanted to get rid of whatever happened to him; he wanted to get rid of those moments, he wanted to wash everything off his mouth, his body, his mind and his soul. However, he felt them clenching it further and all he did was cry!

His childhood had already been ripped apart by the monster and he closed his eyes under running water while wailing, “Mama... Papa... Where are you? Why did you leave me?”

Nothing came, nobody answered. Who would?

Saviour

01 March 2003
(09:15 PM)

Bhuvan transformed Suyash into his readily available sex toy after that day. The freak had no regard for the child's physical or psychological condition. It had become almost customary for him to prey on the tiny babe in the woods every other night. That evening was no different and Suyash started wailing the moment his uncle caught his hand.

Khat khat khat... The unprecedented knock shocked both Suyash and Bhuvan.

Bhuvan was frustrated at the untimely intruder and shouted, "Who's there?"

In the meantime, Suyash started offering a thanksgiving prayer to god for the unknown saviour outside the door. He did not have a smidgen of an inkling about the cruel conspiracy that had been knitted against him; about the physical and mental menace, that life wanted him to endure that night!

He was but a child!

"*Main hu... Akki!*" A husky voice came from the outside.

"Hu... Just a minute. I am coming." His uncle shouted back irritated and walked towards the door as Suyash left a long breath out in relief.

That was the first time in the few days that Suyash had been there that someone had come to visit his uncle and that too at that hour, things seemed odd! Why would anyone visit someone that late until there was an acute emergency!

However, those things did not occur to Suyash. He was too young for that. All he knew was that Akki's arrival had prevented him to go through disgust at that time and he was pretty happy about it.

Soon, a man around five and a half feet tall with a sturdy figure, curly hair, three to four day subtle, clad in multi-coloured t-shirt, grey jeans and blue slippers entered the room as Suyash eased himself in the same place while doing his best to remain silent. He did not want anything ugly after the visitor left.

Whenever a person goes through the worst phase of life, things that would have usually gone unnoticed start to matter like hell and sometimes things that a person would have hated to do under normal circumstances start to give happiness.

It was the same with Suyash. He never liked anyone visiting their house during the night, but that day his soul was beyond happy at the arrival of an uninvited guest.

He had never washed dishes or his clothes! Never had he even lifted a finger to do any of the household chores. Why would he? He was a cherished son! He hated getting up early in the morning, but then he started loving doing all of those things as it ensured that his uncle would stay away from home as much as it would have been possible.

He had tried to escape once unsuccessfully, but the result was horrendous. There was a vast expanse of uncultivated field on all sides. The young boy was completely baffled and was unable to identify directions. He kept on moving through the unending fields until found by Bhuvan late in the evening.

Suyash went through hell that night as Bhuvan got his hands on the child weary of running after the escape! What followed was more intense punishments. He made him stand next to the pole fixed outside the house and then tied his hands to it using a barbed wire. He did it in such a way that it wasn't too tight to tear his flesh immediately, but enough to ensure he didn't slip out of it. He had done it to ensure the child had to stand the whole night, deprived of any sleep whatsoever! The moment Suyash turned heavy eyed and mother earth craved to caress the somnolent child in her lap, the unforgiving metal hooks started piercing his soft flesh relentlessly and all the sleep evaded him forcefully by the intense pain. All that came out was squeak followed by a shrill cry that shook the heaven and earth!

Even the ground where he stood was filled with sharp edged metal boulders that was used to fix the pole and they enjoyed biting the tender soles of his bare feet.

The process continued until Bhuvan stepped out of the house the following morning. Suyash had gone weary of crying, standing and of pain, his wrists and sole had sustained numerous cuts! He was barely able to stand and keep his eyes open due to drowsiness and weakness! His hands were covered with dry blood! His eyes were bloodshot and swollen, yet the monster did not have an iota of pity in heart for him!

"Ohh betu... sorry. I forgot that I tied you here." Bhuvan said and acted running towards him in slow motion before reaching and releasing him with a sinister smile, "Don't run away from your uncle, no! See the things that you make me do to you." He kissed his wrists and said, "Go get some sleep and don't do anything stupid. I love you."

The dire condition of the kid did not mean shit to him!

"Arey Akki! How come you are here, now?" Bhuvan's loud voice brought Suyash back as the two men who seemed to be good friends hugged each other.

"Kutch nahi yar Bhuvan. So is this your nephew about whom

you told me?" Akki said with a wicked smile while eying him.

"Yes!" Bhuvan grinned as the two looked at him as if he was a freshly cooked aromatic grilled chicken. Their mouths were already salivating; wetting and blotting out words like humanity, love and compassion from their books!

It really was an emergency for Akki or else why would he paddle his bicycle for more than three kilometres at that time of night!

Bhuvan asked, "What happened?"

"See, I am terribly hurt."

"What? Why?"

"You call me your friend and then you have all the fun alone." Akki said.

"Naa... It's not like that. I...." Bhuvan stammered when Akki interrupted him, "I am sorry, but I cannot let you have all the fun alone tonight!"

"You are welcome to join me brother!" Bhuvan replied.

"I knew you were not going to disappoint me. *Tu mera sachcha bhai hai*," Akki said and hugged him.

"*Bas bas*," he said while pushing him away, "But do you think he can endure the two of us. He seems to suffocate and die while satisfying me."

The two of them laughed proudly while appreciating their individual manliness while the child was struck with an inexplicable terror. He had realised the intentions of the incumbent! He wanted to run away, never to return, but there was nowhere for him to go. He closed his eyes and recoiled again. He started praying to be saved. But this is *Kalyuga*!

"Don't worry! I don't need to suffocate him. I need something else!" The evil in his voice would have shamed the worst of demons and it shook the child much more as he continued praying vehemently with folded hands and closed eyes!

"Pray pray, may be Lord Krishna will come and save you." Bhuvan mocked and they started laughing outrageously!

"Let's start the *Vastra-Haran*!" Akki said.

"Sure! But you were saying you need something else?" Bhuvan questioned.

"Yeah... yeah... you will come to know all about it soon. Let's do first things first." Akki replied and the two hefty humans walked towards the ten-year-old kid to mash him up as he trembled and sweltered profusely. Even his voice ditched him.

Too much to be true

01 March 2003
(09:35 PM)

The child screamed in horror as the monsters neared him. He did not know what was going to happen to him. It could have been the last night of his life and he tried to run through them, but was caught.

"You want those!" Bhuvan pointed towards the pile of unforgiving sticks again.

"Nooooo!" He shrieked, "Please leave me, uncle..."

"*Alle...* by now you should be used to it." He said while caressing his head.

The two friends looked at one another and Akki replied, "Don't worry child. I am not going to do anything like your uncle. Your mouth is too small for mine."

"What do you mean?" Bhuvan's ego was hurt, but they laughed loudly the moment Akki winked at him.

"You first take care of your uncle. He deserves the precedence. Then you shall get the chance to be blessed by me." Akki said proudly and they laughed again as the kid cried continuously.

He had no choice, but to do what he was told to and it was not long before the helpless child lay there on the floor, pale and lifeless as Bhuvan continued fidgeting with his toy, still yelping with pleasure.

"Wow! That looked awesome." Akki exclaimed.

"Yeah." He replied with a wicked smile.

"I suppose he isn't dead?"

"I don't think so. He is the son of a tough guy." Bhuvan winked and they laughed together again!

He had pushed the child way beyond limits that evening, hurting his entire orifice! Suyash was still motionless as blood-stained semen dropped out of his mouth.

"There is blood. Did you ejaculate blood Bhuvan?" Akki shouted.

"Nope." He saw the clear drops on the floor and said casually, "He must have got a cut in his mouth."

Suyash did not get 'a cut' that night. The child had sustained scores of cuts in his tongue, gums, inner cheeks and throat!

He regained sense only after a few minutes while the monsters were busy sniggering! He got nauseas the moment he sat up and threw up immediately.

"What the fuck is this, you pig?" Bhuvan shouted.

"Just chill bro... Don't give him a heart attack before I get my $#*&@ on him." Akki said and the two started laughing again as the child spat blood while accepting his fate wordlessly!

01 March 2003 (10:32 PM)

Akki said, "My turn now..."

"All yours..." Bhuvan replied looking towards the kid.

"I will take him to that side. It's dirty here." Akki said and dragged the slender structure of the child towards the other corner of the room.

The child had turned absolutely silent. He wasn't even crying anymore because he knew that there was no way out for him. He was preparing himself for what was about to come: more bruises inside his mouth; the pain and burn that he was about to undergo;

a much filthier and unclean phallus to enter his mouth; for that hateful sticky fluid to be released inside his mouth and all over his body; to be choked nearly to death again; to feel nauseous and then puke again and again; for that tremendously yucky taste and smell to stick permanently to his body and his mind.

He had no idea that something much debauched awaited him!

"Hey, Bhuvan! I can't do it in front of you. Can you give me some privacy?" Akki requested.

"Okay sister," he replied and said, "Make it quick, if you can. I will make a drink."

"I can do anything no?" Akki asked.

"Just don't kill him." Bhuvan looked into his friend's lust filled eyes.

"Okay boss." Akki replied and Bhuvan left the room while closing the door behind him.

That was the first time in their life that Bhuvan's presence was missed by Suyash. He realized that he was feeling safer when Bhuvan was around and started yelling, "Uncle, please don't go. Don't leave me here with him."

Fear of the unknown with an unknown person gripped him and he started banging on the door.

Nothing came except for Akki with a stick in his hand. Suyash fell down in fear and opened his mouth as a sign of submission. He did not want anything remotely like the one he faced a few days back. Akki seemed to have no effect and swung the stick with full force. Suyash closed his eyes and shouted in anticipation of extreme pain, "Aaaaaah....!"

Baam...! A loud clatter muted the child immediately.

He started crying, but soon realized that it had not been used against him.

It took him all the courage that he had to open his eyes and was shocked at the sight. Akki had used the stick on himself. He could see drops of blood and a thick red mark of the stick across his chest and shoulder.

He hit himself once again; this time in clear view of Suyash. *Baaaam*

The child was horrified. It was much harder this time; he even saw blood drops splattered across the floor and wall. Suyash was dumbfounded as Akki struck himself once again with all his might and a malevolent smile on his face. Drops of blood reached the child's body as he cringed in horror. He wondered what that man was up to?

Akki then looked at the stick and took out some of the skin that had glued itself on the stick while enjoying the pain with an acute sense of satisfaction, "Aaaaaah yessss!"

He then looked into Suyash's eye and said, "If I can do this to myself, just imagine what I can do to you."

Suyash had never seen anything like that before. He was shaken to the soul. His uncle seemed a much better person to him and he wanted to get into his lap. He remained mum as Akki started removing his lowers right in front of him.

He was disgusted, but his eyes refused to close. His limbs failed him that night. Dead silence ruled the room for the succeeding minutes as Akki pierced his own thighs with the razor pointed stick.

The image was too much for the boy to bear, and he closed his eyes tightly as blood poured from the stick's sides.

Akki groaned in pain and pleasure, "Aaaaagh...!"

A few seconds of dead silence was suddenly followed by a sound of water trickling somewhere near. Suyash did not dare to open his eyes until a stinky breath hit his face along with some warm fluid under his body. Suyash was absolutely repulsed by the sight in front of him! Akki was completely naked, squatting and urinating right in front of him! "Why are you doing it here?" He asked him while getting up reflexively to dodge the warm fluid.

"Shhhh..." Akki hushed and signalled him to remain where he was. The child looked into his bloodshot eyes and fear turned him into a statue! The obnoxious smell filled his nostrils as the urine mixed with blood wetted Suyash's butts and thighs.

Akki unexpectedly caught the child's shoulders tightly who was still oblivious to what was about to follow and looked blankly into his eyes that radiated inexplicable evil.

The big man pushed the child down to make him lie prostate and shouted "Lick it!"

"Mmmm.... N... N... N...." The child tried to speak as Akki rubbed his face on the wet ground!

He tried to resist as he shouted again, "Do it you fucker!"

"I... I... caa..." Suyash tried to speak, but was pushed harder.

"Lick it now dammit!" He shouted seemingly getting into an inexplicable sensual black hole!

Suyash was in a lot of pain as his face was crushed by the increase in force. He was left with no option, but to follow him and he did!

The psychopath released the child's urine soiled face, picked up the stick and started piercing it in his wound again! Suyash was horrified; he was shaken as the maniac closed his eyes and groaned loudly!

Suyash stared at him in dread and the next moment the monster opened his eyes, showed the stick that he was using on himself and roared, "Enough of your fucking drama. Are you going to finish that or you want this in your mouth and ass hole and all over your body. I would enjoy even that!"

The terrified child bent down mechanically and started licking the repugnant fluid like dog.

"Oh yessss... Yesss... Finish it off." Akki started groaning. He then clasped that stick hard so that it pierced into his palms and he started bleeding more. The blood soon dripped down the stick as Suyash slurped all of that blood mixed with lewdness and his tears!

He wanted to vomit numerous times, but gulped everything in due to horror.

"Don't stop... Yesss child.... Do it." He sighed and clasped the stick harder to enjoy the pain. Suyash wasn't released until every single drop on the floor was inside him!

* * *

The child was in the bathroom, trying to puke out every drop of disgust in his body as the maniacs continued drinking and laughing preposterously inside. Tears refused to stop even as his eyes got swollen up and turned red. All of his internal organs felt like being churned in a grinder. Cruel unrelenting hiccups made things worse. Every part of his body was in agony!

He cried unrelentingly for hours until he could no more and then shouted at the top of his voice, "Enough is enough!"

That became a moment of paradigm shift for him. A new feeling took over all of his disgust, hurt, pain and sorrow. It was hatred; intense hatred! Something he was nowhere near aware of until then!

He stopped crying and wiped his tears. The little man had already made a decision; and he didn't care about the consequences. He washed himself thoroughly and waited patiently until he could hear them talk no more. They had been nattering continuously and silence meant only one thing – they had passed out.

The child gazed towards heaven with a heart that was overflowing with rage! He walked in through the unlocked door, wiped his tear and mud spoiled face with his palm and looked around hurriedly. His exploration ended as he caught sight of the axe that seemed to call him out raucously. A sinister smile clenched his lips as he walked towards it slowly, but unwaveringly. He picked up the axe that had been sharpened just a day before by his very own Bhuvan uncle.

He then dragged the weapon into the room where the psychopathic monsters lay serenely after annihilating the child beyond reparation. His body shook vigorously and sweated profusely as he ogled at his preys and the axe in a row.

He did not waste a second further. Disgust and fury fuelled him sufficiently as he shouted at the top of his voice and struck Akki's neck with whatever residual strength was left in him. Blood gushed out immediately, but he did not yell. The man was tanked entirely and Suyash hit him repeatedly until the head fell off!

He then sauntered to the other side of the bed, where Bhuvan snored unconsciously without an iota of hint of what had happened or what was about to recur. Suyash shouted at the top of his voice yet again and repeated the gruesome act.

The bodies of Bhuvan and Akki had sixty-three cuts apart from the blows to their necks!

The kid then tottered to the other room and sat down, shakily gawping his blood-spattered face, hands, and body. The brash quiet of that dreaded night was crammed with his earth-shattering wails, "Mama... Papa..."

New places, new beginnings

12 November 2004
(11:00 PM)

A few sorrowful months passed in the correction centre; there however had not been a single day when Suyash had not asked himself, "Was I wrong?"

He often wondered why the judge sentenced him, even though the crime by the deranged monsters was evident. Even a doctor stamped his claims; yet all of those were not reason enough for him to kill those bastards!

Time is a great healer is an age-old proverb and all the burning questions, the feeling of guilt, the loss – everything that added to his agony faded with time as he got accustomed to the new place that was cut off from the entire world. Even though life was tough, he got attuned to it soon; above everything else, he was slowly getting happier. At least he didn't have to face what he had faced every other night!

The last night in that god-forsaken house continued giving him nightmares for a very long time. He used to get dreams of the horrendous things that he underwent and that was always accompanied by reveries of lots of blood oozing out of Bhuvan and Akki. The trances were not only limited to bed time; he shouted at any time of day as if undergoing the abuse and would cover his face as if to prevent splashes of blood from staining his face! He also got nightmares of those two men taking the form of evil demons; torturing him to death. He saw them hanging on top of him, whispering things in his ears and reaching out to fuck him again! Although the judge had ordered for psychological and medical help for him, nothing showed up!

Every other night he would get up petrified, shouting at the top of his voice for help. It was then that two of his inmates, who were a couple of years elder, supported him in an incredible way. They gave him water, tapped his head and told him some hilarious stories to help get over!

On some of the days when Suyash was extremely frightened, he would request one of them to share the bed with him and they were always happy to oblige! The two little souls did whatever they could to comfort him!

It is really startling how we find love and support in the places we expect it the least. Suyash was one of those lucky guys who found love that he was craving for in the most unsought for place and where it is unexpected, the jail!

However, it looked as if fate was utterly displeased with the child's newfound happiness and ensured it did not last very long. The Correction Centre was closed due to some administrative issues and all the children were shifted to different places. Suyash was the most unfortunate one as he was sent away alone.

The night before separation, the three friends shared the bed and talked to each other the whole night, promising to go against all odds to stay together once their terms were over; and on the day of transfer, they hugged each other and cried before they were made to depart forcefully!

It was then again time for fate to smile as unhappiness loomed large in Suyash's life.

***

Suyash was startled to see that all the inmates were far more elderly and seemed extremely rowdy, in his new dwelling area.

"*Naya murga aaya...*" Someone taunted as he moved towards the cell assigned to him.

"*Naya aur chooooota sa murga Kuck du koooo...*" Someone else said and everybody laughed raucously.

"Shhh...!" The policeman who was guiding Suyash hushed them and they giggled covering their mouths.

"Yum yum...!" Someone slurped and he was again unable to locate who did that. He was fucking scared! The little boy had no idea that he was in no Child Correction Centre; he was in a real prison!

He had been through such hell in the few days with his uncle that life in the previous place seemed akin to heaven. Though he never stopped missing his parents, the void was insatiable!

But then, it was again time and hell found its way back to Suyash! A strong negative vibe crawled like a vicious serpent into his head as he entered through the strong iron grill. The intensity was sizeably more than what he felt with his uncle! Nothing and no one seemed friendly like the previous place. Even the policemen were extremely rude. He wanted to go back. He wanted his family. He prayed for at least one of his friends or at least someone his age, but the idea that eluded him was that we have to surrender ourselves to fate because there is no way out. It seemed as if destiny had decided for Suyash's life to be a bed of thorns! It was just that he was a kid and wasn't prepared for that kind of harsh realities of life.

Suyash was extremely anxious as he looked around at all those terrifying beings. He felt surrounded by hundreds of Bhuvans and Akkis! That was the first time he cursed himself for killing them. Thoughts of his life possibly being less scary with his uncle clouded his mind, followed by spiritual thoughts of that being god's punishment for the double murder that he had committed. The judge had sentenced him to five years in a juvenile correction centre, but maybe it was god's decision to put him in that place!

It is an un-contradicted human behaviour that crisis kindles the usually dormant spiritual side. Suyash who had expurgated all connections with the Supreme Being for being separated from his friends started praying fervently for protection, "Please protect me, god. Please save me. Please be with me." It however appeared that the place was actually *forsaken by god!*

He longed for company like the one before; the company of his friends Govind and Rishab, but his cohort there was an indifferent adult man who was just over five feet tall, had a long beard, a big belly and a big cut mark in his right cheek. He looked dangerous and Suyash did not have the guts to get anywhere close to him or even utter a word in his presence.

Worst was at hand

21 November 2004
(11:00 PM)

Suyash's butts were glued to the farthest corner of his bed, where he was shedding tears over his misery and missing his friends Govind and Rishab. Just then, some indistinct voices caught his ears. He was frightened to the soul and got into his blanket immediately. He peeked through a small hole in it when the voices seemed dangerously near and saw a few scary people entering his cell. His partner got up at the clang and asked, "What do you want?"

"We have nothing to do with you. We are here for him." One of them said while pointing towards Suyash.

"But he is just a child." The man said timidly.

"So?"

"Please spare him."

The other person smirked, "Just shut the fuck up!"

Suyash was already trembling in fear. He knew they had come for him. Everything that had happened to him when he was with his uncle got freshened up immediately.

Are they here for the same? The thought made his head spin in fear.

"Please god. Save me. Please..." He started praying again when someone pulled the blanket off him.

He shouted stridently in his terror, "Nooo...!" and one of them hushed him, "Shhhh...!" and laughed, "Why are you shouting kid?"

Another man caressed his trembling body and said softly as if trying to console, "Don't be afraid child." But the child started howling more the moment that man raced his fingers on his body, "Please leave me, somebody save me... help... help!"

The first man said, "Shut the fuck up dammit. Although there is one thing we would like you to know, you can shout as much as you want son. Nobody's going to come and save you here. So, I suggest you save your strength."

All others started laughing. The time with Bhuvan and Akki suddenly started to seem much more tolerable to the child at that moment. Four people stared at him with lust dripping uncontrollably from their eyes. He was absolutely cognizant of that look at a very early age (it wasn't supposed to be that way). He just didn't know how to protect himself.

He dragged himself further away from them, as if trying to push himself into the walls if that was possible. Just then the men reached for him and tried to get hold of him as the child tried to fight them off. He ran hither and thither and even bit one of the men. It was then that he received a heavy slap that dazed and rendered him wobbly. That moment was enough for those brutes to immobilise the child. They caught his limbs firmly and ripped off his pants almost immediately.

The group then forced him to kneel down on the bed. One of them then pressed his head down on the bed while the other one pushed the two pillows under his belly.

The child was then positioned perfectly for the act and one of them took the chance to hold his hips strongly so that they did not slag down on the ground and his ass would be readily exposed for them to exploit.

Suyash just kept on resisting without knowing what was

about to follow.

"What's this?" One of them growled looking at the small glass container with yellowish petroleum jelly.

"We did not find Vaseline this time. We got this."

"Hmm... It seems good." The first man took some of that greasy jelly on his palms and smelled it.

"I hope it would work better."

"Yeah... Indeed!"

The first man put a handsome amount on his shaft and then took some on his fingers and inserted it in the child's asshole.

Suyash got an extremely weird feeling as the finger rotated all around his anus. He even started getting some burning sensation immediately. He knew what was about to follow and increased his resistance to free himself. However, the struggle just drained the energy out of him. His strength stood nowhere near those three hefty men who did their best to keep him immobile.

Baaam! A heavy hand on his butt made him cry in pain and took the remainder of his energy away.

"The more you resist and move, the more it shall pain child. The choice is yours." The first man laughed and others joined him.

Suyash gathered all his strength for the last time and tried to move when he roared, "As you like it!"

He caught hold of his butt and pushed his lubricated tool inside the greased asshole of the child, which was torn apart instantly. Suyash cried in inexplicable agony while his thrusts became harder. The monsters did not display any mercy whatsoever!

"Stop... stop. I can see a lot of blood." One of them said after a few minutes and he stopped at once.

"What the fuck?" He shouted and retracted himself immediately. A huge amount of blood gushed out with it right away. They had not expected that to happen. They were terrified as the child's awful wails shook the prison's bars.

The four men ran out of the cell, threatening Suyash's cell partner, "You will get much worse if you tell the authorities about it."

Suyash's cell partner started shouting at the top of his voice, "Help, help. Please help the child or else he will die."

Everyone in the neighbouring cells who knew what was happening started shouting loudly for help. There was a big commotion and the guards rushed in to find the ruthlessly sodomized child who lay motionless, bathed in his own blood!

Rashid's Lamentation!

There, my baby, my loving nephew and my only family was being dragged cruelly through fire and thorns and on the other hand I was busy in my own life crammed with ignorance, self-pity and guilt.

The memory of Suyash's birth on the 22 August, approximately two years after my sister Bushra and Niket got married was as fresh as morning dew in my mind (and is still the same now). I was elated beyond words, but my mountain sized ego prevented me from visiting them. I was angry at my sister because she chose a Hindu guy!

Niket and Bushra had fallen in love while they were pursuing their grads from City College, Raipur and got married soon after they completed that course without any major obstacles. Both of them had lost their parents early in life and had started shouldering their younger brothers' responsibilities, namely, Bhuvan and I, Rashid, from a very young age.

Bushra started to work part-time in one of the local garment shops soon after our father passed away. Our mother had already succumbed to a major complication during my birth! Our parents were orphans; hence we did not have even a distant relative to take up our responsibility. All our neighbours looked after us enthusiastically for a few days, but started to ward off slowly with time.

I always respected my sister for whatever she did for me, but never approved of her marrying Niket! For me, he was just another Hindu guy who would convert my sister into a Hindu and keep her like a maid! I never knew the source of that feeling, but I am so happy that I was wrong. He was a good man; actually, the best my sister could have got! But I realized that only after everything was over.

As sick it may sound, but the fact was that I used to keep a close watch on Niket and his activities, because I loved my sister a lot and did not want her to get hurt. However, I stopped it after a couple of months as it felt stupid and I did not find anything against the man.

That should have been the time to insert myself in the family, my only family; but my ego disallowed.

She must have been missing me just as I did because she visited me a few times and I hushed her away rudely; just to satisfy my fucking ego. I feel so ashamed of myself!

But love started to take over bit by bit soon after Suyash was dropped from heaven. A small get-together was organized to celebrate the christening ceremony of the child and both Bushra and Niket came to my place individually to invite me. Every cell in my body and soul pushed me to be a jubilant participant in the service, but I allowed my ego to take the reins yet again. I went there only to fulfil the formality.

Bushra was thrilled to see me visit them and Niket's face reflected intense gratitude the moment our eyes met that day! I was overly surprised to learn that the child was named as Suyash Ijaz Krishna, as a symbol of communal harmony and I realized that I had been all wrong about Niket. Nevertheless, I was too proud to admit that openly.

That was the first time I saw Suyash and I fell in love with him immediately. I think that's what 'love at first sight' means!

His dark brown innocent eyes seemed lit up the moment he saw me and his giggles became a reason for my smile from then on.

I still remember the serenity that was instigated by his touch as he caught my index finger and covered me all over. I was mesmerized beyond description and had goose bumps everywhere as Bushra put him in my lap. Never before had I held anything that small and tender in my arms. I was nervous, extremely excited and felt butterflies fluttering in my belly!

The infant had started loving me from day one! He did not cry in my arms like in everyone else's.

I still remember that Bushra had a big smile on her lips when she said, "He likes you already Rashid!"

"I love him so much." I wanted to say, instead I stared at one of the most beautiful creations of god in my arm for a few minutes; kissed him when nobody was seeing me; whispered in his ears, "I love you little man. We are going to do great together!" and gave him back to Bushra before leaving the place soon after.

That was one of the biggest chances for me to make everything good; but I was stupid. As a matter of fact, I got a plethora of chances even after that. My sister and brother-in-law both wanted me, but I chose to remain distant. How I regret it every day now? I should have enjoyed a full family when I had a chance to, but I always promised myself, "I will do it tomorrow!" and that tomorrow never came!

I never visited their house after that day. However, I met Suyash regularly almost every day. His parents were well aware and did not raise any objection whatsoever. They knew that I treasured him and they were happy that Suyash was loved by his uncle! Moreover, I loved to gift him things and in my mind I wanted to spoil him, although in a good way.

Both Niket and Bushra used to invite me whenever they planned a family outing and I walked away wordlessly. What a fucking idiot I was!

It is a harsh fact that life doesn't give us too many opportunities and foolish people like me waste those willingly just to regret later!

I learnt that in the harshest way possible when I went away from my beloved nephew for a few days. It was during the New Year of 2003 and I went on vacation with some friends for the first time ever.

However, by the time I came back, the most wonderful thing in my life, my beloved Suyash and my entire family was long gone. I had lost everything I ever had; everything was finished!

How many times have I wished to go back in time and undo my vacation, thinking that maybe things would not have happened the way it happened if I were there! How many times since then have I wanted to undo at least one of those fucking actions that I had taken to hurt my sister! But...

I had come back with a bag full of gifts for Suyash – toys, clothes, gadgets, eatables and what not? But he was nowhere to be seen. I learned that Bhuvan had taken Suyash to his ancestral village, but I had no idea where that place was. I had never been interested until then! By the time I started enquiring, it was already very late!

A tape can change your life

My life had turned topsy-turvy and was filled with negativity after the dreadful incident that took away everything from me. I had started to raise questions on my existence in this life and even tried to finish myself! The only reason I backed off was a small hope that may be someday I would meet and bestow my love on Suyash. I did not know then that destiny had other plans!

I was surrounded by a lot of people, yet was absolutely alone. Everything seemed strange and all I did was pray for Suyash's well-being; although it was only later that I knew that all my prayers had been summarily rejected by the Supreme Power.

I usually strolled in the vicinity of that empty house where they used to live and imagine the three happy souls as I used to see them while shedding tear. Suyash's sweet and childish voice in which he said, "Mamaji" whenever he saw me reverberated in my ears every now and then. The mere thought of him made me howl in my agony. I often saw him scuttle towards me to hug me tight like before. I would tighten myself for the impetus, but all I caught was air because it was just in my head.

****

On one of those days, I went to a shop that rented video cassettes as I needed something to distract me, even if for a few minutes!

"*Ramesh bhai... Woh waali video tape dena...*" I meant porn and he understood it. It was always available, but only for those whom he knew personally.

He eyed me top to bottom surprised, "*Waah... Pehli baar Rashid bhai!*" His look made me doubt my own decision. But I needed a distraction and that seemed like a viable option.

"Haa... Haa... *Kutch achcha dena... naya...*"

"*Tumhare liye toh saara hi naya hoga...*" He chuckled and winked.

"Offo..." I said with a plastic smile.

"*Hmm... Yeh maine bhi nai dekha hai... Kal hi aaya hai... Le ja maje kar... Mere taraf se pahli baar tere liye free...*" He said and wrapped it in a brown envelope.

"Thanks, brother!" I said and left.

***

I hit the play button of my video cassette player and shouted at the top of my voice, "What the fuck?" I was shaken to the soul and ripped out the tape and burnt it immediately.

That was the video of my sister crying and stripping her clothes!

"No... no... no..." I started thumping the floor with my feet and punching the walls uncontrollably until I was able to do no more and sat down beating my head and my chest with my blood-stained hands and cried continuously. Even the walls were tainted red by then!

I slapped myself a hundred times while bleeding from my nose and mouth and did not stop even then. I had committed a great sin! I then stood up and hit my head against the wall with full force and fell down dazed with a thud.

I passed out momentarily and prayed to Allah for forgiveness on regaining senses, but I was unable to forgive myself. It was only after days of whimpering and inflicting self-pain that I reached a saturation point while a lot of unanswered questions hovered in my mind:

Did it happen on the same dreaded night?

Who made her do that?

Who was responsible for the detestable act?

What else do I not know?

I had realised by then that there was something more to the story than what was known to me. Although I had tried to get hold of the people who might have been involved, but had found nothing. It seemed that they had vanished into thin air. But now that I had seen that video I knew that there was a great chance that I was missing something really big!

That was when I decided to dig deeper and took a solemn oath to find those bastards and make them go through hell on earth before they met the maker!

It was then that I used my contacts with 'the different set of people' whom I had befriended working as a contractor in real estate world. Their work system, networking and information was impeccable and gave me results sooner than I had expected. However, the shocking revelation of Bhuvan, Niket's brother, who had taken Suyash's custody made the world around me spin. It was the damned Bhuvan who had come to the aid of that drunken couple, Mr and Mrs Tamang who wanted their revenge. They managed to slip out of the lockup after bribing the police and went straight to Niket's house. Bhuvan guided them all through because he wanted them to kill his brother so that he could become the sole owner of the entire property and they were happy to oblige! He had no threat from the child whom he wanted alive for personal reasons. He however didn't care what they did to Bushra! Further, he also helped them leave the town after committing the ghastly crime.

The grisly info was akin to a big rock that crushed my heart and filled my mind with appalling apprehensions concerning Suyash. A person with that kind of heinousness could do anything to the child! He could molest him, sell him for a few thousand rupees or even kill him! The possibilities were unending.

I filed a complaint in the local police station against him and waited restlessly until I received the news of an unconfirmed location, yet again from the 'other set of people' and I waited no longer.

A million negative thoughts that was mildly soothed by the belief of seeing Suyash stormed through my mind as I raced towards the destination. I kept my fingers crossed, hoping that I wasn't too late. However, my apprehension multiplied manifolds as I stepped in to the village and enquired about Bhuvan and Suyash to the inhabitants. They knew the notorious Bhuvan and also about his brother Niket. That meant that I was in the right place. They also confirmed seeing the child with him through the photograph that I had carried along with myself. Nonetheless, the worst part was that nobody wanted to talk about it. They were frightened that a curse might grip them if they said anything about what had transpired. However, they did point me towards the house that was located far away from all others in the vicinity.

* * *

An awful stench hit my nostrils the moment I stepped in through the door of that cursed house.

"What kind of hell is this?" I murmured nervously while looking around for his trace. The place looked filthier than an unmaintained pig sty!

I stepped inwards towards what seemed like a bedroom and was stunned. My legs gave up immediately and I dropped down on my knees. The walls of the house started spinning at an unimaginable speed and I threw up immediately.

The next moment I shouted, "No... No... No!" and started crying bitterly. I knew I was late; as a matter of fact, I was exceptionally late. Every inch of the place was sullied with dry brownish-blackish blood that was being feasted on by flies and insects. There must have been much more before because the ants were busy carrying it away.

The sight was too much to bear and I ran out immediately and puked. The stench had bolted itself on my nostrils and the sight denied leaving my eyes as did the tears.

"No... No! That cannot be Suyash's blood!" The very thought was more dreadful than my worst nightmare, "That was too much blood to be of a kid." I tried to pacify myself.

But I needed answers. I needed to know what the fuck happened there, and more than anything else, I needed to learn the whereabouts of Suyash.

I noticed the crowd that had gathered approximately a hundred meters away from the house and strode towards it for answers. However, everybody but one dispersed by the time I reached them. He spoke even before I asked anything, "*Bahut bura hua bachche ke saath sahib.*"

"*Kya hua?*" His tone took half of the life out of my body.

He then told me about the crime scene and murder. He also told me about the child's verdict and every word the man spoke was like a spoon of highly concentrated acid thrust into my ears, burning my whole body inside out. I started wailing in inexplicable angst!

A few other villagers joined the scene as they saw me crying. Conversation with them revealed that they used to hear faint sounds of the child screaming in agony on most of the nights, but they never dared to check the notorious Bhuvan!

Cowards! I thought. *What else did he do to you son? I am so sorry; I was not there for you.*

I had never felt that helpless until then, but all I could have done was shed tears in front of everyone.

I asked them, "*Suyash kahan hai abhi?*" One of them replied, "*Usko police waale le gye...*"

I did not waste a moment and rushed to the nearest police station, but they had no record. There had been a massive explosion, just two days back, in one of the suspicious trucks that had been seized and parked in the premises of the police station. It had resulted in an uncontrolled fire that had turned everything into ashes and dust, including a lot of lives! All the policemen involved in the child's case were dead and I was at a dead end. It seemed that an unknown force was working extensively to ensure that I did not find my beloved child! But it had to do much more than that to keep me down.

I was not going to give up until my last breath.

***

It took me a long time and a lot of effort, but I was eventually able to locate him at one of the Child Correction Centres located almost a thousand kilometres away from our city. Nobody knew how he got so far! I arranged for and reached the place the very next day. However, bad luck laughed vociferously at me again as the same had been shut down due to some administrative issues. I tried to get hold of the children's list and the places they had been transferred to, but got nothing. I did not find his name anywhere and I was at the impasse yet again. Destiny had its own agenda that it needed to fulfil before allowing the disclosure of his location. However, in our case it was more of the police officers who had their own set of hidden agendas!

However, I was not there to give up. I made new contacts and threw huge amounts of money hither and thither to finally see my nephew in a Central Jail. The bastards had sent him to a full-fledged prison. I also learnt about all the brutality he had endured and I knew that I was very late, once again!

The Present

Everything has a price

8 February 2019
The Oaktree Restaurant: Raipur,
Friday, 08:00 PM

Rashid finished his recitation in utter quiet. Kanika's heart was filled with sorrow for the guy she adored, Suyash. The tears from the two sets of eyes soaked the cloth of the table on which they sat. However, Kanika was a smart girl and she still had doubts lurking in her mind and she wanted clarification for the biggest one. She said, "But I still don't get as to why you told me all of this. None of this justifies his lying to me and it doesn't even reveal how you know my parents!"

Rashid gestured to say when she interrupted him again, "I think you were just wasting my time. I suddenly feel like all of it is your mind's creation!" Her sympathy suddenly took the form of irritation.

She started questioning her decision to enter the restaurant. If she had not seen the car and had not stepped in, everything would have been the same as before. She would not have had to listen to Suyash's painful story. If any of that was true...

She even felt that Rashid had cooked all that just to reinforce sympathy for Suyash. Maybe they had a different agenda altogether! She was confused and did not know what to think and thought that it was better that she hopped off. She stood up jerkily and then sat back down with a final question, "Just tell me what the fuck has anything that you puked on my face got to do with me? I need nothing more."

Rashid puffed out a big lump of air noisily and said sarcastically, "It has everything to do with you girl!"

"I need full answers. I need to know how you know my parents. This story was a complete waste of time. I doubt if any of this was even true." She said rigidly.

"Every word is true and I can show you some concrete evidence if you agree to come to my place for your answers." He said, looking straight into her eyes.

She gazed deep into his old eyes and tried to assess as she had been trained to as a recruitment expert. *His eyes do not look like that of a liar.* She thought as he got up and asked, "So?"

Don't do it Kanika. It's a bad idea. You don't even know him. A voice inside her head said as she got up perfunctorily. Kanika was not using her brain. She was cheated, hurt and had a strong urge to get the answers. It hushed all other voices and made her follow him mechanically.

"Get in." He said while stepping into a grey SUV.

She saw Suyash in the driver's seat. She was broken and irritated, yet she felt abundance of love overflowing for him. Things that had transpired in the last hour or so had changed nothing in her heart for that man. She felt cheated and vulnerable, but still trusted him. That's how fragile the human mind is! Practicality changes nothing in a moment! Moreover, sympathy had taken the steering and she wasn't going to stop.

A feeble whisper tried to warn her again, *Don't Kanika.*

"I want to know..." She said to herself, closed her eyes and got into the car, although with a plethora of doubts.

***

After a one-hour trip through tough terrain and terrible quiet, the car came to a screeching halt in front of a two-story building. Kanika made a point of entering the names of all the small towns they passed through on her phone, in addition to making mental notes of the big shops, markets, and other notable landmarks! However, her efforts turned seemingly futile as the last twelve to fifteen kilometres were nothing but vast stretches of dry fields!

"Where are we?" She asked looking towards Rashid while stepping out. Suyash left the place with the car immediately after dropping them. "This is Suyash's ancestral land where we built this new building a few years back." He replied and signalled her to follow.

The place looked deserted and could have been very well what he said it to be. However, she did not find a single house on their way! Things were turning out to be daunting!

She asked, "So this is the very place where Suyash had killed his uncle plus one?,"

"Yes," Rashid replied.

"But you said that there was a village somewhere around. I don't find anything around here?"

"Yes... You may find remnants of some houses on the other side." He said pointing towards a direction, "The villagers started hearing painful voices all night after the incident. They believed that this place was haunted by the spirits of Bhuvan and Akki. Even a few mishaps occurred soon after which reinforced their idea and all of them abandoned their homes and shifted to a different place in their horror."

"What kind of mishaps are we talking about?" Things were getting scarier for her.

"Inexplicable deaths, attacks by their ghouls and people getting lunatic, kind of mishaps. But you don't need to worry about those. We have been staying here for years now. You are safe from the ghosts." Rashid assured her.

He is just trying to fool you Kanika. A voice in her head said. Moreover, Kanika herself was not convinced with whatever Rashid had conveyed and said, "Okay, let's forget about the spook show and give me my answers."

"Of course, You will know everything in a while."

Kanika had started regretting her idea of being there already. The place actually seemed godforsaken and she felt threatened. Moreover, the terms like haunted, ghosts and inexplicable deaths added to her horror, even though she didn't believe in those things!

"What if numerous people with weapons emerged inside the house?" The thought made a big lump in her throat that she managed to gulp in with extreme difficulty.

She thought in continuance as Rashid knocked the door, "They can easily hide my dead body anywhere around here never to be found. This was a very bad idea!"

Her mind went on an overdrive looking for something she could use for self-defence and caught sight of a pile of sizeable bricks right around the door. That seemed to be a perfect weapon to hit Rashid and someone else before escaping, just in case.

Her heart pounded heavily as a middle-aged man who seemed like the caretaker opened the door and she sighed in relief because she realised that she could have taken down both of them if needed!

"*Aaj iss waqt malik* (Today at this time sir)?" The man asked.

"*Haa... Kutch jaruri kaam tha* (Yes... Had some important work)." He spoke and signalled Kanika to follow her in.

Kanika stepped into a big sitting room with nothing, but a cane sofa set and a centre table right in the middle of the room, apart from a dozen plastic chairs neatly arranged at one of the corners. There was an LED television and a music system on one of the sides.

"Please sit down!" Rashid said while pointing towards the sofa opposite to where he sat with a big sigh. His old bones were definitely hurting after the ride.

Khalid came back in less than a minute with two glasses of water and asked, "*Chai ya coffee?*"

Rashid looked towards Kanika and she answered, "I need nothing, but answers."

"*Mast kadak wali chai banao Khalid... Aur fan chala dena.*"

A few silent minutes passed as Rashid tried to loosen up his body via a few mobility drills while seated on the sofa. The only sound that pierced through the silence was that of the speeding fan and the pendulum of the big wall clock!

Kanika was busy sipping the water, while closely watching everything in the room that might be of some help to her in case of an emergency. Soon, she located some firewood, ropes and an axe resting in one of the corners. There was everything she could use and her mind worked speedily to recall the karate moves she had learned during her school days.

It was then that Rashid got up and went inside, hopefully to step out of that room with some useful info for Kanika. At the same time Kanika sought it as a perfect opportunity to bring that axe under her sofa. She was about to make her move when Rashid arrived with an old folder file in his hand.

Kanika flinched and thought, "Damn, I got late!" as he threw the papers in front of her!

"What is it?" She asked, perplexed.

"You are educated enough. See it for yourself!" He replied sarcastically.

She rolled her eyes at him and opened to find a few old papers.

"I don't understand." She scattered all of it and said, irritated looking at all of it cursorily.

He sat down beside her calmly and pointed towards an old pic, "Do you recognize them?"

Kanika looked at it and realised she had definitely missed that and exclaimed, "Yes! But?"

"Yes, this is Mr and Mrs Tamang."

"What the fuck are you talking about? They are my parents." Kanika shouted as her eyes widened with every passing moment, "Wait... wait... you want to frame my parents for murdering Suyash's parents?"

"You see this paper, Kanika. This is the photocopy of the FIR that was registered on the day of the accident against the Tamangs."

He threw out some more pics from the folder and threw it in front of her, "These are your parents. Isn't it Kanika?"

"Yes, they are but these are so old and..." She stammered and was interrupted by Rashid immediately as he continued, "These were taken by the neighbours and also by Suyash's father on the day of the accident!"

"These are your parents, Kanika – Komal and Arisha Tamang who changed their identity and became Kunal and Kriti Chettri after committing the heinous crime and then vanishing. They did not just murder, but also made my sister strip in front of a camera before raping her and making the same video again. Further, as if that was not enough, they sold the same in the open market. I don't know how many millions of people might have seen her naked until now! Every part of her body was put on public display. What the fuck were they thinking? They destroyed a family, my only family, completely and what for? Just for money... They don't fucking deserve to live."

Kanika was unable to believe anything that she heard and saw right then. She was not ready to accept the allegations against her parents. She knew that was a blooper because she knew all about her orthodox parents and started crying, "I think there has been a mistake. My parents are nothing like that."

Rashid replied, "There has been no mistake Kanika. They are nothing like they appear to you. They destroyed a family in a single night for their revenge. And now they are going to experience first-hand how revenge tastes when it is served chilled."

Kanika didn't know how to react and reiterated, "You are mistaken. They cannot be my parents."

"It took me years to track them; and my sources are unimpeachable." Rashid said with an unprecedented air, "Suyash was already in his job by the time we came to know about you and your placement and planned everything. How do you think you ended up in Raipur when you could have been posted anywhere in the world?"

"What do you mean?"

Rashid replied, "It was Suyash and his contacts, teamed up with some of my sources, who ensured that you get posted here."

Kanika was knocked for a six, to know that they had planned her posting.

"But why? Even if I agree for a minute that they were my parents, what do you want from me? You say you traced them... so?" She threw those questions on Rashid rather boldly and extremely defensively, but numerous apprehensions already rendered her shaky, "Are you planning to gang rape and kill me?"

"Or are you planning to make a video of me while processing all of the above and make it viral?"

Her thought was interrupted by Rashid's not that bold voice, "Because your parents are going to pay for what his parents suffered and you will have to suffer for what Suyash had to suffer!"

The man grinned and Kanika knew she was in some deep shit. Maybe it was time that her apprehensions were going to take an ugly shape.

However, she was not going down without a fight and shouted displaying falsified courage, "What do you mean that I will have to suffer?"

Rashid smiled cunningly, "Do you think we planned everything just for nothing?"

"If you want to kill me; I suggest you get over with it now." Kanika repeated the dialogue of an English movie that she had watched a few days back without giving heed to its meaning.

"No lady, not at all... If we wanted to kill you, he could have done it in your place or anywhere else? Why bring you here?" Rashid's voice was ice cold.

"Then why am I here?" Kanika was trying hard to act unflinching while readying herself for action at an opportune time.

"Actually, you being here happened only because you wanted to surprise Suyash and that was not in his plan. You weren't due in this place until tomorrow evening." He paused for a moment and continued with a smile, "But anyway, everything happens for a reason. Thanks a tonne because you made things easier for us by agreeing to join us."

"You are never going to get what you want." She shouted and was about to leap towards the axe when someone very sturdy caught her from behind and put a handkerchief soaked in chloroform over her mouth and nose.

A few seconds passed before she lost her consciousness.

"Put her in that room!" Rashid said to the young man.

"Hmmm..." He said and carried her away!

PART- II

Prologue 2

Suyash, Govind and Rishab were partying in Rashid's house in Raipur. Rashid's unalloyed efforts had made it possible for him to track and bring the three friends who had met and developed an unbreakable bond in the Correction Centre together.

Suyash had told him about his pals who had been with him during the darkest of days and wanted his uncle to find and bring them. Rashid, who was ready to go to any lengths to make things better for his beloved nephew did not leave a stone unturned to re-unite them!

The trio were having one of the best times of their miserable lives when someone knocked. Suyash went to take the door and shrieked.

Govind and Rishab ran out to find half a dozen goons and a gentleman. Suyash was on the floor and one of the men had his boots pressed against his chest and a gun on his head.

"Who are you? What do you want from us?" Rishab cried.

The neatly dressed gentleman pointed towards Govind and replied calmly, "Your friend knows!"

Rishab's eyes were then fixed on Govind who was struck by the biggest horror of his life. He was shivering like a dry leaf as his eyes met the vilest person known to him.

"Is this Seth Manek Lal?" Rishab asked and Govind nodded his head in confirmation.

"It's great to know that your friends know me!" Sethji smiled and continued, "*Arey Govind beta...* when did you step out of the jail? You did not even come to meet me. That's so rude of you *Gobi.*"

Even Rishab and Suyash quivered in fright as they knew all about the richly clad demon in human form.

Sethji said again, "Say something beta."

The words were followed by a deafening silence; a type of silence that would shake even the most eclipsed ear. Govind gathered every iota of courage in him and asked, "Why are you here?"

"I am here for you son."

"I am not your son."

"That is so rude, especially after all I have done for you." Sethji smiled cunningly.

"You took away everything from me, you monster." Govind did not know from where he got the audacity to shout at him.

"Well, I did, but it seems you got new things." He said while pointing towards his friends.

"I don't even exist for you. Please don't do it!" Govind went down on his knees and pleaded while rubbing his head on Sethji's shoes in horror.

"Hmm... You know, I really want to get merciful and stuff. But there is a big problem!"

"What Sethji?" Govind continued crying.

"You exist and I saw a smile on your face. I am sorry but I cannot let that happen. Every time you smile, I am going to take it away from you. You are not supposed to smile or be happy in this life son." He said and signalled the man who had Suyash at gunpoint and a deafening gunshot turned everything silent in less than a nano-second.

"Nooooo...!" Govind shouted and leapt towards Sethji, but was hit by someone on his head hard and he fell face down with a shriek! The whole room was sprayed red and all he saw through his hazy vision was a motionless Suyash a few feet away from him. Tears broke all barriers, but he wasn't even able to shout.

Sethji then motioned his eyes towards the dazed, frightened and paralysed in fear Rishab and the gun-man fired two continuous shots at him before he could have attempted to lift his foot up.

Rishab fell down with a thud and turned silent after whining in agony for a few minutes.

"So Govind beta... Remember and be careful before you smile the next time." Sethji said coldly while looking into his eyes and left the house with his men.

Govind's friends lay still in front of his eyes! Suyash's head was splattered in to pieces! It was a point-blank shot. Rishab's body was motionless, soaked in blood!

Govind shouted at the top of his voice, gathered all the residual strength in his body, picked up a knife and slashed his wrist!

The whole room turned into a pool of blood. The red coloured life force of the three best friends mingled together as one!

Govind's eyes were still open as his past life painted its picture in front of him!

The Past

A small wonderful world

Year 2001

Govind was like all other carefree kids around him who attended classes in government schools more for a one-time meal rather than education. He was least interested in schooling and all allied stuffs. However, he was not even inclined towards the miscellaneous activities like fishing, swimming, cricket, kabaddi etc., akin to the boys of his village.

He was the one and only little man who was genuinely interested in Shalini or Shalu, as he called her. The love of his life!

He had known her since as far his memory took him. She was Seth Manek Lal's daughter; the very same person who had employed his entire family. His mother used to baby sit Shalu while also looking after petty works in the kitchen; his father supervised the gardeners and other house keepers who worked day and night tidying Sethji's bungalow that was named as *Lal Niwas.* The periphery was spread over hundred acres and included a large building, staff quarters, a parking space, a beautiful garden with a large variety of different flowers, dairy farm, printing press and various other plantations that included but were not limited to mangoes, guava, banana and teak wood. Seth Manek Lal was one of the most powerful civil contractors of the state who bagged almost every work that he eyed! He had colossal stacks of money and very deep political connections. There was an office outside the living area of the house where Sethji used to take care of all his works.

Sethji was so riveted in making money that he had no time or intention to allot even a diminutive portion of his life to his daughter Shalu. Unfortunately for the little girl, her father's way to express love was through materialistic gifts (that she never wanted) and he believed that the luxury that he provided her was more than enough to fill the void created by his absence in her life; even if it didn't, he didn't bother.

Her mother was always busy with business meetings, outings and parties and never had time for her since infancy, hence pushing her further away with every passing day! The ridge between her and her parents grew wider as they got busier making money and enjoying late night parties that were often accompanied by extremely late mornings.

Shalu could be considered one of those ill-fated patrician girls who never found a hero in her dad or a friend in her mom! She used to crave for them in the initial years of her childhood; however, the indifferent attitude of her parents soon made her lose all interest in them! She stopped expecting anything except fancy clothes, toys and video games!

Every mislaid relationship; especially the ones that have love and expectations attached to its very core; gives rise to a sizeable vacuum that craves for satiation! Shalu was no different. This emptiness in her life was initially filled by Govind's mom whom she used to call *Amma*. However, with the passage of time that need was satisfied by Govind, whom she called Gobi, and who became her best friend!

It had become a routine for the two young souls to rush back from the school fleetingly just to meet one another. Gobi didn't even bother to change; neither did Shalu; nor did anyone in the world give a fuck.

Their fondness for each other nurtured exponentially with their age; however, what they did not realise then was that they were no longer each other's want; they had turned in to each other's need which was taking the shape of obsession out of their knowledge!

They were unable to bear any separation, so much so that Shalu started rejecting foreign tours during vacations so that she could stay at home and spend time with Gobi, whereas Gobi stayed with his parents the whole day in the bungalow so that he could be near her.

The entire world of the two young in-love souls revolved around each other as they studied, played and ate together.

"My mother, Mrs Snehkumari Lal, would not mind Gobi eating a couple of chapattis from her kitchen Amma," Shalu would say every time to ensure that he ate with her.

The fact was that Shalu's mom, never cared what went on in the kitchen. She had never set her foot there except on the first day after her marriage when she had to cook food for her in-laws to fulfil the needs of tradition. That was the last!

All her meals and snacks as per her demands were served either in her bedroom or packed to be eaten somewhere else. The big posh *maharaja* style dining table in the middle of the hall was just a means of showcasing landed gentry, remaining unused for most of the time and for instances when some bureaucrat or a political leader was invited for dining with Seth Manek Lal!

Shalini never had a memory of having a meal with her mom. She doubted if that had ever happened. She, however, did remember having occasional breakfasts with her father in the drawing room before going to school, even then he was either busy over phone or with his secretary or something, that was of no value to the young lady!

There was a time not long before when she craved for Sethji's attention. It was that dire need that motivated her to study hard. She got sweet fruit of her toil and secured first position in the class. That turned out to be one of the most happening days of her life. Her name was announced in front of the whole school during the morning assembly. She received her report card from the hands of the headmaster along with a small prize. Wishes from other students and teachers continued until she left the school.

However, things were bound to change inside Lal Niwas! That was the first night that she waited for her father and rushed towards him as he stepped in when the clock struck eleven!

"Dad!" She exclaimed with a big spark in her eyes and put forth the report card and the prize.

"Yes... Why are you up until now?" He asked while still looking at some of the papers in his hand; completely oblivious of his daughter's words.

"Just see this dad." She said louder to get his attention and pointed towards the column that stated *Rank 1*.

"Good!" He replied indifferently and walked away towards his office with his secretary while talking about some deal that they needed to grab!

Shalu was stunned! She had imagined a lot of appreciation, hugs, kisses and chocolates; but what she got was an uninterested *Good* before he got busy in his work in less than a second. All her labour to get some attention from her dad went in vain. She had already given up on her mom until then! That day, the little girl was heartbroken and made a silent sobbing pledge to herself, "I will never do anything to win his attention. I'll do everything for myself." He didn't care, and she didn't care anymore.

There is only one friend

"*Teri toh lottery lag gyi yaar...*" Shivesh taunted Govind after school hours while they headed towards their home (actually Shivesh headed towards home and Govind towards the bungalow).

"*Kyun?*" Govind looked at him with questioning eyes.

"*Arey... Itte bade ghar ki larki pata liya,*" he said with a wicked smile.

"*Aisa kuch nai hai*" Govind tried hard not to blush but failed miserably.

"*Achcha... toh humse bhi milwa na... Itti garma garam maal hai... thora hum bhi toh chakhe.* Bring her to meet us. She is damn hot." Laxman who was walking just beside Govind said and the two started laughing.

The words set Govind on fire and then something happened. He punched Laxman right on his nose. The boy fell down yelping as he held his nose that had started bleeding profusely.

"*Pagal ho gya hai kya?*" Shivesh shouted while aiding injured Laxman.

"He got it because he behaved like a dog!" Govind shouted and ran away.

"*Ja ja...* You hit your friend for a girl. We will see you!" Laxman shouted while wiping his nose and groaning in pain.

The fact was that they were never his friends. They were just known faces that lived around and studied in his school.

Govind had only one friend, Shalu and that friend had turned to something much more, something beyond what he had imagined!

He reached the bungalow in the next ten minutes, went straight towards the tap in the garden and put his right hand under the cold running water.

"Aaaaahhh...!" He sighed in relief as cold water flowed through his hand and kissed the ground.

He had been successful in hiding the acute pain that had originated in his knuckles and had moved towards his fingers and upwards towards his wrist and forearm after he punched Laxman hard.

Minutes later he was in the kitchen and asked his mom, "*Shalu kha li kya maa*?"

"Has she ever eaten without you?" His mom questioned him back.

"*Naah...*" He said with a smile.

"Go and tell her. She is waiting for you only," She said.

Jiffy, and he was in front of her door. He was about to knock when she opened the door, "What took you so long today haa?"

"Nothing, Guruji asked us to clean the class room before leaving, so..." He said while trying to ensure she didn't get a glimpse of his right hand that had swollen much more by then.

"Okay, Okay... I get it." She said while interrupting him in between, "But, what are you hiding behind your back?"

"Nothing. Let's go and eat. I am starving." He answered hurriedly.

"Gobi!" She said sternly, "What is it?"

He knew he was busted and couldn't hide it anymore and showed it.

"Oh my god!" She shouted, "How did it happen? This looks bad."

"I got hurt by one of the desks while moving it." He lied straight to her face. Revealing the real cause was against the unsaid and unwritten bro-code!

"Shit! Come inside. I will put some spray and crepe bandage." Shalu tried to take him by his left hand.

"No no... I will be okay." He said.

"Gobi! Now stop acting like a donkey and come on in." She said dominatingly leaving him no way for refusal. He knew that she wouldn't take it!

He stared at her lovingly as she applied some spray on the swollen area before wrapping it with a pink coloured crepe bandage.

Apprehensions

Govind's head was filled with numerous questions the entire night, even when he wasn't thinking about Shalu! Sleep was a million miles away from his eyes. *Why do I miss her so much?*

Why do I feel like I need no one else but her in my life?

Why do I feel lifeless until I see her every day?

Why can't I stop thinking about her all the time?

Why... Why... Why...?

The lad tossed around in his bed restlessly with zero thought about what had transpired that day with his so-called friends. There had luckily been no issue with Laxman and/or Shivesh until then.

However, that also meant that Govind would have to be ready for their strike; anytime and anywhere. The game was on!

But was Govind really a game? Not at all. He was just a simple boy in love, pure love that was devoid of any kind of iniquity associated with money, caste, creed and any selfish motive whatsoever.

The school boy, who had been rummaging for the answers throughout the night was successfully able to relate his condition to one of the Hindi movies he had seen a few days back before the first ray of the sun warmed the surface of the earth. The hero of the movie had the same symptoms as he and was finally diagnosed with the disease of *love*!

"Damn! I am in love. I am in love with Shalu!" He said to himself as the golden beam lit up his room softly.

* * *

That moment was like a point of *nirvana* for the child and resulted in a radical change in his appearance and behaviour. The pleasant erudition that morning had made his mind step through that supple sunbeam and float among the clouds ecstatically. His subconscious mind further gave him an unmitigated access to all the love songs that he had heard since his childhood days. One after another and then another, he sang them continually.

A pleasant smile had made a permanent dwelling on his face twenty-four hours a day after that pleasant realisation which turned into some serious blushing business in the presence of Shalu. He even started paying very close attention to his dressing that was comprehended by everyone around.

His parents were absolutely aware of the reason behind that change; however, they chose to ignore it and laughed at it in each other's company, thinking it to be an unattainable fleeting infatuation of the young boy. They did not have a slightest clue at that time that they were categorically off beam.

However, Shalu, who was the sole reason for Govind's transformation, was completely bewildered at the sudden change in Gobi's attitude. It was mostly because he had started to avoid her most of the time unless they came face to face.

So, one fine day, she stood in front of his mother and asked, "*Amma*, may I ask something?"

"*Pucho na beta.*" She did her best to veil her smile as she had a pretty good idea of what her question might be.

"*Yeh... Gobi ko kya hua hai?*"

"*Kutch bhi toh nai... kyun?*"

"He seems changed to me."

"I don't know... ask him only." She replied pointing towards the garden where Gobi was busy removing the weeds from among the flowers.

"Hmmm..." Shalu answered and went straight to him, "Hey Gobi!"

"Hi Shalu!" He replied his gaze still fixed on his work while all his senses were focussed in her.

"What are you doing?"

"Nothing as such. Just..." She interrupted him and said, "Forget what you are doing, come walk with me..."

"But father has..."

She cut him short, "Leave it and come."

He left the things as they were, washed his hands and joined her in her walk.

"What's going on?" She asked him.

"What do you mean?"

"You know exactly what I mean. Don't act stupid."

"I really don't understand what you're talking about." Govind replied with an innocent look on his face, although he knew what she meant. He had been struggling hard to face her for the last few days. He wanted to be with her, yet he rushed away nervously and confused upon seeing her. The little man had very little idea that he wanted to redefine his relationship with Shalu, but was unable to do so!

"Uff... You have been acting really strange for the past few days."

"Strange, as in...?"

"Strange as in... you are not making eye contact with me, you are not talking to me properly. You come here right on time but you don't sit with me. What's going on haa?"

"Is it? I didn't realise." He looked to the other side.

"Really, don't try to act smart Gobi. I am smarter than you. Just see! You can't even look into my eyes and your eyes tell me clearly that you haven't slept properly. You never used to do the stuffs like gardening; rather you always preferred to sit and chit chat or study with me. So quit beating around the bush and tell me the matter."

Govind did not have the courage or an ornamental set of idea or sentence at his disposal at that time to respond; however, he also did not have the audacity to walk out on her without answering. As a matter of fact, a big part of him wanted to tell her everything, but the other part was completely against that idea!

Furthermore, he had never refused to do anything she had asked him to; after all, her family was his bread and butter! *Should I tell her?* He thought as Shalu said, "Gobi, stop thinking and give me an answer. I need it."

Just go for it you stupid. It's now or never. A voice inside shouted at the top of its voice.

"I am sorry!" He paused momentarily and murmured after a few seconds while looking away from her, "But I think that I am in love with you!"

"I didn't quite get you." Shalu said sternly, "Can you be a bit loud?"

"Okay... okay. I think I am in love with you. I love you Shalu." That time he said it loud and clear, looking straight into her eyes. Although that was not how he had planned to propose her. As a matter of fact, he had never thought of proposing her.

Sometimes (or it can be safely said that most times) it's just on that nick of time that the things happen; just as destiny had planned it; and it was one of those times.

Gobi then closed his eyes and prepared himself for the physical and mental abuse that might be unleashed on him, but something entirely different happened.

"I love you too, you idiot!" Shalu replied instantly.

"Wh... Wha... What?" Govind did not believe what his ears had heard and asked, "What did you say?"

"I said that I love you. I love you very much Gobi."

Govind hadn't expected that kind of response from her. His eyes were still wide open and his thoughts went blank. All his senses were paralysed!

"What happened? Why did you turn into a statue?" Shalu asked him.

Her words brought him back to this world and he said, "Really?"

"Yes Gobi. I have always loved you; only you were stupid enough to have realised it now."

"Really...!" He was still trying to get hold of reality.

"Yes Gobi! I love you." She said, looked around to ensure privacy and kissed his lips.

Govind was completely unprepared for anything that transpired, but reached seventh heaven in no time. He embraced her tightly!

A lot of hormones kicked in immediately as the two young teenagers smacked each other's lips amateurishly. Govind was getting out of control within a few seconds and started kissing her hard.

"Ouch! Easy tiger!" Shalu said and he replied with a "Sorry."

"Don't be!" She said and they kissed again like they had seen in the movies.

The two very young souls in love enjoyed their proximity to the fullest, absolutely oblivious of the outside world en masse.

Bitterness

Around 10:00 PM

Govind was lying on his bed, suffering from pleasant insomnia after an unprecedented day. He was on cloud nine. The incomprehensible feel of her tender lips coated with a luscious aroma of cherry had cemented itself to him. Her fragrance was lingering in his breath. The sensors in his palms had inexplicably locked her texture in all its brilliance. He was physically away from his love, but his mind was imprisoned in that moment and his smile deferred itself indefinitely leaving ever since!

It was around ten and his parents had already dozed off after a hard day's work.

"Mangilal, open the door." A rough voice coupled with a loud bang spilled a lot of black coffee over his white spotless thought process.

Govind got up irritated and walked to the sole bedroom of his house that was used by his parents. He said, "Baba... someone is banging the door."

Multiple rough voices hit his ears and shook him, "Mangilal, you asshole, you fucker, are you dead? Open the door!"

His father who was dead asleep recognised the voices and jumped out of the bed to get the door in less than a minute.

Baam! A tight slap made him kiss the ground, "Aaaah!" and spurted out all the remnant sleep from his eyes painfully.

Govind and his mom ran towards the door on hearing him gripe.

"*Hai...? Kya hua ji? Kyun maara inhone aapko*?" She was shocked to see him on the floor and started crying immediately.

Mangilal stood up the next moment trying his best to veil all the pain and fright through his half-hearted words of confidence, "*Kutch nai?* They are our masters. It seems there has been some misunderstanding!"

"There has been no misunderstanding!" One of the men said and stepped forward to hit him again when Govind came in between. None of those hooligan-like men looked like *maalik* to him. Although a child, he knew that those crooks did not resemble the gentle and peaceful Seth Manek Lal even marginally.

Govind shouted at the top of his voice, "Who are you? What do you want?" And realised his mistake immediately. He started trembling vigorously as all eyes shifted towards him. It was then that he saw over a dozen huge men. Govind had even missed the huge number of cars parked right there with scores of men!

"Shut up Govind! This is a matter of elders." His father pushed him out of harm's way.

One of them shoved Mangilal away and grabbed Govind by his collar, "Is this the boy Sethji?"

Govind was scared to death and tried hard to free himself, yelling at the top of his voice, but the goon was too strong for him.

Govind's mother ran and caught that man's legs as Mangilal cried with folded hands, "He is just a kid sir. There has been some big misunderstanding. Please sir... please leave him."

The despondent couple then ran towards Sethji to beg for mercy, but were stopped by a couple of armed men as Shalu's father, Seth Manek Lal stepped out of his car.

"Yes, this is the one. Hand him over to the police." He roared ignoring the wailing parents.

Govind was shocked to hear Sethji's voice that evening. He was dead frightened. His hands and legs gave up and he went mum.

Both Mangilal and his wife got down on their knees immediately with folded hands and said, "Seth ji, please tell us. What happened Sethji? What did he do? He has always been a good boy."

Govind was still trying to get a grip on the situation. He tried to think what wrong he had done, but his brain failed him miserably.

"Ask your son? What he did?" He roared again.

Mangilal turned towards him and asked, "What did you do Govind?"

He looked at him blankly. He had no idea and said, "I don't know baba."

"Really, then what is this?" Sethji signalled and one of his men fixed a miniature battery-operated television on the hood of the car.

One of them connected a video tape and Sethji roared, "Check the video, you mother fucker!"

His men surrounded the TV with their backs towards the screen so that neither they nor any other person could see it. Govind was dragged near to it and the world toppled upside down for him. It was the video of him and Shalu hugging and kissing each other!

His legs turned shaky and gave up immediately. He fell down asphyxiated with no idea how that happened. He wriggled on the field to get some breath. His parents wanted to reach for the child right then, but both of them were restrained.

They continued crying and shouting at Govind's dire condition and thought of what might follow. His mother feared the worst and freed herself somehow and ran to her son. Govind had regained his composure to some extent until then and his mom first hugged him and then started slapping him, "*Yeh kya hai Gobi?* Did I give you birth so that you may show me this day?"

She did that to satisfy Sethji. She was terrified he might kill him in his rage; even Mangilal mirrored his wife's action the moment he was released.

The couple then fell down at their malik's feet and started crying for mercy, "Please forgive him Sethji. He is just a child. We will send him away from here. All of us will leave this place forever. Please forgive us Sethji."

"How dare this bastard touch my daughter? Not only that, someone put this tape in my bungalow. There might be copies of it. Do you think I can let this go just like that? All my name and fame has been jeopardised because of this fucking boy!" He said and kicked Govind, who was still trying to regain his shivering on the ground. He cried in agony as he received a few more kicks from him.

After hitting him for a few more times he shouted, "Inspector sahib..."

A man in *khaki* came running and said, "Ji Sethji..."

"Take him and ensure that he doesn't come out soon!"

"Ji Sethji." He said and signalled a constable to pick and put Govind in the police van.

"Please have mercy, please forgive him Sethji. He is just a child." His parents kept begging.

"The only reason that he and you are alive is because I am having mercy on you Mangilal. For the things that you have done for my family; but from now on, forget about your son. He will be alive but never with you. Consider your requests granted." He said and got into the car.

Just before leaving the place he lowered the window and said, "The two of you don't need to come to work from tomorrow."

The cars sped away, filling the place with an impenetrable cloud of dust as his mom kept crying inconsolably on the ground while his father ran behind the vehicles!

11:13 PM

Govind's mother was still weeping when her eyes were dazzled by bright lights of a few cars. She recognised it to be Sethji's immediately and ran towards it with all kinds of positive thoughts in her mind, "May be Sethji's heart changed and he decided to act mercifully. May be he did that just to fill fear in Govind's mind and then when he was absolutely terrified, he decided to return back her son to him."

But then there was a thud and she shrieked in horror.

Her husband's body was thrown out like a sack of waste right in front of her feet. She fell down on the ground and put her husband's head on her lap and started rocking his blood-stained body, "Please get up, what happened to you?"

She was aghast at the horrendous truth that was unveiling itself at its own pace. Mangilal was barely breathing when Sethji stepped out of the car and said, "Did you really think I would just let it go? The two of you are equally responsible for everything. Did you assholes really think that you insects had a chance at my daughter? You don't deserve to live and I will make sure that your piglet will endure hell on earth."

The bereaving mother and wife gave no heed to his words. She had already fixated death for her entire family right then. Her husband was already breathing his last and his son, who was nowhere to be seen, was already assumed dead by her. There was nothing left for her to live on in that life and she prepared herself for the same.

The wealthy monster however misunderstood the silence of the angst-ridden lady and shouted, "You mother-fuckers!" and kicked the woman on the face and yelled again, "Lock these bastards inside and put their house on fire."

None of the damned villagers raised even a finger to help as the group of earthly demons cremated two live people in their presence. The lady's heart-rending shouts should have melted any human heart, but nobody came to help.

That was not it; the monster had ensured that everything transpired in Govind's full view. So, he was right there; hanging motionless with his hands cuffed to the police van; fully conscious but unable to move due to the intense beating that he had received along with his father just two kilometres from his house!

His life had transformed from being picture perfect to a complete mayhem in a matter of minutes. It had been not more than two hours, that he had been enjoying some of the most beautiful memories of the day after having a heavy dinner and some jovial chit chat with his parents. And then there he was; already an orphan; an orphan with torn skin, muscle tears, tendon damages and multiple fractures all across his body.

* * * *

The child had endured a lot already, but the fact was that was just the beginning. The nastiest demons of hell were prowling close ready to devour him; slowly and painfully. It was in an effort to unleash those fiends that a false case was registered against him.

It was said that he tried to rape one of the girls who worked in Sethji's house. A girl, whom Govind had never seen in his life was brought in the court to give a statement against him!

The lawyer further added that Sethji did not file a police complaint then because he was just a kid. He let him go away with a warning. However, Govind, who should have been ashamed of his act, did not exhibit any sort of regret and went back home enraged.

Everybody in Sethji's bungalow had assumed that the kid would get back to normal and mend his ways after he had cooled off. However, there was no way they could have foreseen what occurred back in his house. He had a heated argument with his father and blamed him for everything and when his father tried to make him understand, he lost his mind. Govind then picked up a spade and hit his father multiple times and also injured his mother who tried to stop him. He then locked them inside and put the whole house on fire. When the neighbours tried to stop him, he started beating everyone with the spade in his hands, injuring a few of them. All the injured people were presented in the court, who gave statements against him.

It was when things went completely out of hands that people called the police. Govind even attacked them. It was in the series of those attacks to which the people and the police tried to defend themselves that he sustained those injuries. Even the judge was Sethji's friends and did not pose a question regarding the critical and life-threatening wounds that looked nowhere near being endured through self-defence actions!

All odds were against him and he was charged on attempts to rape a minor girl, injure over a dozen people including policemen and, above all, for murdering his parents. He was also ordered to be taken to the mental asylum to get assessed for his psychological condition.

He was then taken to the psychologist, who was heavily bribed by Sethji and certified him to be mentally ill. He furthered that he was extremely dangerous and posed a grave threat to the life of people around him and should be kept in confinement for treatment. In accordance to the reports, Govind was admitted to the mental hospital where the demons started to prey on him unswervingly.

He was forced to undergo unimaginable torture in the asylum at the directions of Sethji. He cried and shouted and gnashed his teeth in agony with no one to listen as he was administered shock treatment every two to three days, without any anaesthesia, as mandated by Sethji. The burn, the pain and the intense cruelty of the people inside was unbearable for him. He could smell the sweltering blood in his veins each time and wanted to finish himself to get rid of the pain. However, he was bound in chains in a way that rendered him immobile and he had no choice, but to endure all of that.

The child was given medicines that made him hallucinate. He scratched the walls until his nails came out and still didn't stop. Drugs were administered so that he could inflict more pain on himself by peeling the skin off his flesh and bite the iron rods until his teeth fell out.

Soon, all of that coupled with endless shock treatments turned a perfectly healthy boy into a lifeless pile of bones and skin! He didn't even have the energy to eat on his own, leave aside doing anything to kill himself.

All he did was pray in his heart (because he did not have the strength to move his lips), "Please take my life god. I cannot take this anymore, please!"

These things continued for over six months after which Sethji might have gotten some mercy in his heart and he ordered for him to be sent to jail.

The day he was released from the asylum was by far the best day in Govind's life. He thanked Sethji a million times in his heart for the mercy that he had shown; regardless of the fact that he was the only one responsible for slaying his family and all the torment he had undergone.

That is yet again a harsh reality of life. It makes us feel grateful for the stuff that seems unbearable to others. How many of us feel going to a prison is good? Zero.

But the child was more than happy!

Govind was then transferred to the Child Correction Centre where he first befriended Rishab, who had been sentenced a few months before him, and later, Suyash.

Visitors

The Correction Centre seemed like a heaven to Govind after those horrid days in the mental asylum. It was purely a miracle that he had neither lost his sanity nor his life after what he was made to undergo in that godforsaken place!

The nightmares, however, kept haunting him for months! He became insomniac and trepidation had glued itself to the deepest corner of his heart and though life had been comparatively very peaceful for him in the new place, he feared it to be just a beautiful dream.

He feared that he would find himself back in the asylum if he closed his eyes! He got into a foetal position whenever he saw any of those guards stepping towards him. The sight of ward boys in the previous place dragging and strapping him onto the bed before passing electricity through his body mercilessly, were refreshed every time. The burn, the pain, that hard black ball plugged in to his mouth, the cuts in his lips and tongue each time, nausea, constant vomiting, severe headaches and losing himself for hours every time.

At times, his mind would imagine all those hard-hearted doctors who administered him with painful injections that was followed by the most dreadful hallucinations. And every time that he got back in to his senses, he found himself in intense agony with scratched face and body, nail-less fingers, broken teeth, torn skin, deep bites anywhere on the body and much more!

Everything, literally everything crashed on him like a giant rock pushing him back to the life that not even the most cursed child was supposed to live!

However, one of the caretakers in the Bachcha jail, Nilesh Bhatt, somehow developed a soft corner for the child and helped him get over his past along with Govind's partner Rishab. It took him months to start getting back to regularity, both mentally and physically.

It was there that on one of those days when he had more or less recovered, his old friends from the village, Laxman and Shivesh showed themselves. He was never happier to see anyone else as he was that day. He was seeing a known face for the first time after a very long time and although their last interaction had ended with a fight, all of that seemed to have been things of previous birth.

He had given up all hopes in that life, but it was as if things had started to get in line for him.

"I have never been happier to see anyone else my friends." Govind said the moment he saw Shivesh and Laxman in front of him.

The warmth, the pain in his heart, the nostalgia and the memories associated with Shalu, everything dawned on him instantly and brought tears in his eyes. Even though it was a Bacha Jail, there were bars between them and all he could do was shake hands with them.

"How are you Govind?" Shivesh asked.

"I am okay only... what else can I say? I am alive and breathing." He said dolefully and asked them, "What about you guys?"

"We are good!"

The answer hurt Govind badly. Even he was supposed to be good. Even he was supposed to be on the other side. Even he was supposed to be a lot of other things that they were and he was not. However, he put on a plastic smile on his face as his heart wailed in agony and replied, “That’s so nice to hear.”

“We brought this for you.” Laxman gave him a packet of his favourite *besan ke laddoo.*

“Thank you so much yaa.” He said and started crying as he put one of it in his mouth, “It has been so long.” and again his tears choked him.

Those laddoos took him back in time when his mom used to prepare it for him at home. It was his favourite and his mom was famous all across the *basti* and even in Sethji’s bungalow for preparing the best of those!

“Don’t cry buddy.” Shivesh said while caressing his hair through the cold iron bars.

“How is Shalu?” He asked.

“We don’t know. We just heard that she was forced to leave the country. Have no idea where she is now!” Laxman replied.

“Does she know what happened to me?”

“I am not sure, but my mom told that she had a big fight with her dad regarding you. A big scene was created by her in the house, but I really doubt she actually knows what happened to you and your parents,” Shivesh replied.

“Hmm... How would she even know? That monster would never tell her what he did. I always considered him to be a *devta,* but he is the worst *daanav* known to mankind.” Govind said while controlling his sobs and continued, “Do come to meet me sometimes. It feels good to see known faces in the world that has become freakishly unfamiliar!”

“I don’t think you would want us to come to you after hearing what we have to tell!” Laxman’s words changed the atmosphere in a jiffy.

“What do you mean?” He stammered. He was nowhere near ready for another shock.

Laxman answered, "We came here to apologise!"

"Why on earth do you want to apologise?" He said confused and his heart rate had already reached its maximum capacity until then.

"That day my mom had told me to go to Sethji's bungalow to get some mangoes to prepare pickles as per his orders. So, I took Shivesh and Dharmesh with me for help."

"Dharmesh, as in the photographer of our area?" Govind asked.

"Yes." Laxman answered and continued, "We saw the two of you and hid. Your body language told us that something romantic could follow and we decided to enjoy the same. Things happened as per our assumption except that Dharmesh, who was supposed to go make a video in some party after gathering mangoes had his camera right there. He made a video tape of you two, prepared copies of the same in the evening and gave it to Sethji."

Shivesh took over from there, "We did not object because we were angry at you due to our fight!"

Govind looked at them shocked and dumbfounded as he continued, "We did not expect that Sethji would do what he did. We are really sorry, please forgive us." Both of them folded their hands in front of him by the time he completed the sentence.

Tears ran down Govind's cheeks who was filled with a plethora of known and unknown emotions, the biggest of which was guilt. He did not know how else to react and said, "Thanks for coming brothers!" and went inside silently.

The Present

Gobi is back

11 February 2019 (Monday, 11:05 AM)

Shalini took the intercom inconsiderately while her gaze was fixed on her laptop screen, "Yes Anita..."

Her secretary said, "Someone by the name Gobi is here to see you ma'am."

The name enticed every bit of her attention and she exclaimed brashly, "Who?" She was sceptical of what ricocheted in her ears.

"Gobi!" She smirked, "As he says... Ma'am."

She had heard it right. Anita did mention Gobi. Butterflies started kicking heavily in her tummy and she was dumbfounded.

"Ma'am... Hello!" Anita wondered if there was problem with the connection, "Ma'am... Are you there? Should I?"

The reiteration forced the bewildered Shalini to break her silence and she said, "Yes... Amm.. Send him in in two minutes... No no... five... No... send him in ten minutes!"

"Okay ma'am," Anita said and disconnected, absolutely surprised at her reaction.

On the other side, Shalini had turned extremely nervous mechanically. She did not know the reason, but she had never felt what she was feeling then. "Is Gobi really back?" She thought and called her secretary again.

"Yes ma'am?"

"Anita, please cancel all my appointments for the day." She was already planning her day with him in her head. She did not want any disturbance whatsoever if that person was actually Gobi! Moreover, she was the boss of one of the biggest firms and could get all her appointments rescheduled immediately if that person turned out to be an imposter. However, the chances of that were very low because nobody around knew about her past!

"Okay ma'am!" She said in her regular bold yet sweet voice and disconnected the call.

Her heart started pounding fast, so much so that she could hear the beats bare eared. Gobi was back. Her childhood love... her long lost love... someone who had been snatched away from her by destiny was back.

She rushed towards the washroom and stared at her image in the mirror incessantly. She was blushing like never before. She was both thrilled and jumpy. The fact that he had come to meet her meant that he had not forgotten her, just like her! It was just at the most unexpected time.

"Shit! I look so oily." She said to herself and cleaned her face using wet wipes and applied her BB cream immediately. She then wore one of her Kylie Jenner lipsticks in her handbag and applied some eye liner. She wanted to look her unsurpassed best before facing him for the first time in years and all she had was ten minutes!

She took a good look at herself from all angles in the giant mirror before getting back and making herself comfortable on her extra comfy orthopedically designed rotating chair. She did not want the entrant named Gobi to know that she was extremely conscious and super excited!

Everything of the past came rushing down on her, but she did her best to appear calm and composed.

She was done in nine minutes and forty seconds and kept looking at her watch; the hands of which crawled slower than a snail as if teasing and testing her patience.

Finally, it was time when someone knocked at her door and said, “May I come in?”

The voice made her miss a heartbeat and beads of sweat surfaced as if mocking at the fully air-conditioned chamber.

Ms Shalini Lal, daughter of Mr Manek Lal, who returned from the USA after completing her MBA had joined as the CEO of her father’s company, Lal Infra, just a few months back. Her father had ensured that she did not return to India before completing her studies. He had further ensured that Govind (or Gobi) never resurfaced in her life. But it seemed that destiny had some other plans, or it may have been true vice versa!

“Yes, please.” Shalini showcased extreme ease and indifference while she was extremely flustered within.

A sophisticated young man in grey chequered suit, maroon tie and camel brown shoes with an erudite skeleton watch carried his six feet two-inch structure gracefully through the Italian marble flooring of her office.

Shalini was spellbound. She was nowhere near prepared for that and the only words that left her lips were, “Gobi? Is that you?” All her attempts to not exhibit excitement was flooded in his presence. She knew it was him; the face that had never faded in her eyes looked highly unaffected by time and she could have identified his semi curly hair even from the surface of the moon!

He smiled and said, “Yes Shalu!”

“You look so different, you look amazing!” She turned into a statue.

“And you look the best like always.” He replied with a deep sigh.

She got up and rushed towards him. She couldn't help it anymore and hugged him tight.

"Oh Gobi! I missed you so much."

"And you have no idea how much I have missed you in all these years Shalu."

"I thought I would never see you again."

"Me too."

They both had tears in their eyes. Arduous sentiments that they had believed to have been stonewashed in all those years resurfaced like a strong tsunami, reigniting the love that had strongly stood against the biggest test of time.

Silence talked, as a matter of fact it shouted at the top of its voice as they stared at each other for several minutes that followed.

"C'mon take a seat." Shalu broke the silence and pulled him towards the plush leather sofa that was kept at one of the sides on the chamber.

They sat down and she started speaking, "Where were you all these days haa?" Words dripped out like honey from an overfilled honeycomb, "And what a suit... my god! I am shocked."

"Yeah!" He laughed slightly.

They were meeting after more than a decade, but things still felt fresh! It seemed as if they had met just yesterday!

"Uff! I didn't mean that. I meant where do you work?"

"I am not a CEO like you"

"Shut up, I won't talk if you say things like that." Shalu rolled her eyes.

"Okay, sorry baba," Gobi continued, "Actually I just make little bit of money from share markets, nothing much."

"*Achcha!* But you don't seem to be making just *little bit money*!" Shalu said while stressing on the last three words.

"I don't think whatever I make is anywhere near what you make Ms Shalini Lal, CEO of Lal Infra, one of the leading real estate companies in India." Gobi laughed.

"I am really not going to talk if you bring up the CEO thing one more time." Shalu said and got up.

"Arey! I am just kidding." He pulled her down immediately and made her sit closer to himself.

Shalu looked away from him as he got down on his knee and said, "Sorry, I promise I won't repeat it."

She got down beside him and said, "OMG! Where is that old lousy Gobi? This one seems so dramatic." She chuckled and pulled him up, "Now get up, drama king."

They both laughed and sat closer than before. There was a moment of awkward silence as Gobi watched her locks. She was dressed in a white shirt and light grey trousers. The attire hugged her body smartly, hiding everything within, yet revealing her curves and her perfect figure sexily. He stared into her big deep watery eyes that looked bigger due to the makeup! Her fragrance filled his breath and he was too awe-filled to speak! He was at an uncomfortable proximity of an extremely hot girl and did not want to lose himself capriciously.

He was allowed to be mesmerized, but not jeopardize. Shalu could see he was fascinated and did nothing but smile. She had somewhere wanted to see him like that except that she was herself muffled! The simple boy whom she saw last in second hand school uniform and ruffled hair had turned into a fully grown one heck of a man!

"So, you didn't tell me. Where were you all these days?" Shalu broke the silence that was taking a not that advisable turn in the office. She feared her secretary may drop in anytime and find them in a not-to-be-seen situation.

"It's a long story. I will tell you some other day in detail. You tell me."

"C'mon, I will make myself free for you. Let's have a cup of coffee outside." Shalu did her best to conceal the fact that she had already cancelled all her appointments for the day.

"Sure," he said and got up.

Govind had a lot to say. He had an unquenchable fire in his heart and was a man with a perfect plan!

I don't like messiness

11 February 2019
(Monday, 12:12 PM)

"This place serves the best coffee." Shalu said while sipping the coffee in one of the local cafes.

"Really!" Govind made faces as he tasted it.

"You did not like it no?" Shalu's voice had a pinch of despair. She had brought him to the best café known to her and she felt like a failure. Something that she was not used to.

"I can make better than this... as a matter of fact, much better." Govind said with a confidence that felt synonymous to arrogance.

"Oh really?" Shalu's voice had a pinch of doubt mixed with lots of sarcasm.

"Yup... You have a doubt?"

"Of course, I have doubts. How would I know until I taste it myself? Anyone could say anything to impress a girl like me." She replied with fake vanity.

"Okay! Now that you have said that... challenge accepted. I will prove myself." He said with a flair!

"And how are you going to do that mister?" Shalu asked mischievously.

"Come to my house and I will show you how real coffee tastes." Govind answered.

"So, is this an invitation for me?"

"Yup, if you don't have a problem in stepping into my humble dwelling."

"C'mon!" She smacked his shoulder playfully!

"...and don't blame me, you know a lot can happen over coffee." Govind said mischievously.

"Very funny! Huh!" Shalu laughed it off, but the missed a heartbeat the moment those words hit her ear drums. She turned excited, frightened, sad and guilty all at the same time. But she decided to focus on the first emotion, that was excitement.

* * *

Shalini was in a three-bedroom flat, on the fourth floor of a seven-story building that was situated just outside the vicinity of the city in less than forty-five minutes.

"Wow!" She was amazed at the tidiness of the area.

The sitting room accommodated a teak wood sofa set, a fifty-two-inch smart television, a big home theatre system, some beautiful showpieces and a bean bag. One of the walls had wooden racks that was filled with a lot of books and replicated a mini library!

"Who else lives here?" She asked.

"No one." He answered with a smile.

"Where are Amma and your papa?" A sense of nostalgia engulfed her momentarily as she referred his mom as Amma, just like childhood days.

"They are no more." He replied coldly without making eye contact with her.

She felt a big thud in her heart even though she hadn't been in touch with her for a very long time. All the memories related to her flowed back persistently and a drop of tear found its way towards the floor through her cheek. Some relationships are not at the mercy of physical presence, distance or communication. Shalu had just that kind of connection with Gobi and his family!

"I am so sorry Gobi." She spoke with utter difficulty.

"It's okay Shalu. It's been a very long time. I am over it." His lips lied, but his eyes spoke volumes.

"When did it happen?"

"A few months after we parted." He lied again.

"Shit!" Shalu thought. *Life had been so unkind to him. It took me away from him and then even his parents. I can't even think of the hardships he might have undergone.*

She had tried a lot to learn about them after the 'kissing and video tape episode', but all her attempts failed. Nobody told her anything except for her mother who informed that Sethji had sacked and threw them out of the city. He was furious and did not want to see them anywhere near as that incident had caused a permanent damage to his impeccable reputation among his friends, business rivals, relatives and above all, in his own eyes!

Sethji had made an irreversible announcement the very next day that Shalu prepare herself to fly out of the country immediately. She had a big fight with him that day, but gained nothing. She wanted to stay back for Gobi. Somewhere in her heart she knew that he would come for her. However, she did not even have slenderest of notion about what had occurred and the price that was paid by Govind and his family. Nobody could have imagined what her reaction would have been if she got a clue!

She cried day and night, gave up eating and made it practically impossible for anyone to make her sit on-board in defiance. However, Sethji was adamant and he arranged for and transported her to USA in a chartered air-plane after being administered with anaesthesia.

She still had the uneasy memory of that fight with her dad after which a couple of his men held and made her immobile and a doctor pushed an injection in her veins that put her out almost immediately. The next time she opened her eyes was in a bed that was placed thousands of kilometres away from India!

"Where are you lost?" Govind snapped his fingers, bringing her back to the present.

"No... Nowhere." She stammered and asked "What happened to them?"

She remembered well that they were quite healthy the last time she saw both of them. Her best guess was that they must have met with an accident.

"Let's not talk about it Shalu. Just sit down while I prepare coffee for us." Govind ducked the question and tried to change the topic, "So, how was your stay in Amer–?"

"Shhh..." Shalu sensed his pain and put her index finger on his lips and hugged him. She had always loved him, to an extent that she had never fallen in love with anyone until then. Although there had been a lot of flings in her life, but Gobi had always been locked in the innermost part of her heart that defined love for her!

However, it was one of those times when sympathy overwhelmed all other feelings. Silence ruled once again as they realised how effectively taciturnity communicated!

"*Chalo*... I will make coffee." He said while getting out of her grip.

"Why are you in such a hurry to drive me away... haa?" She rolled her eyes, "Shit! Do you have a girlfriend?" She had assumed him to be single, but suddenly the mere mention of that made her quiver!

"Nothing like that Shalu."

She sighed in relief, ensuring to veil the same from him. However, the reply brought back the lost smile on her face immediately. *Thank god!* She said in her mind and spoke, "Hmm...

First I want to see your house."

"Yeah, why not? It won't even take two minutes."

* * *

Shalu was sitting on the kitchen slab after admiring the 3-BHK flat as Govind put milk on the gas stove.

"That was really impressive." She said while trying to catch a stable gaze at him as he moved to get the coffee and sugar.

"Thanks! Just got it three months back."

"Ooooh... I don't think I could keep my room so spick and span all the time."

He was inclined to say, "You can mess it up any time you want; just like your dad did!" Instead he gave her a pretty smile and said, "Thank you. It's only because I don't have a lot of work to do after the share market closes at 3:30 p.m." He paused momentarily, "Moreover, you don't like messy things around you when your life had been messy. I want everything to be in order." He said while shuddering his shoulders.

"It will be." Shalu meant every word she said because she had no idea how scruffy his life had been and how much more of that he was on the inside. All of that elegance outside was just a mask to conceal the muddle within!

"Amen!" Govind said with a smile.

"This is really good." She exclaimed the moment she sipped the coffee.

"See, I told you." He said proudly and tapped his own shoulder in appreciation.

Shalu found his action very cute. She laughed and said, "You actually surpassed my expectation Gobi. I thought you would be all words."

"I am glad you like it."

A lot can happen over a coffee

"I need to tell you something." Govind broke the silence after a few seconds.

"What?"

He looked in to her eyes and said, "I... I..."

"What Gobi? You are frightening me." She was afraid he might propose once again. She was in love with him, but then she was meeting him after years. She didn't know what he might have become, she didn't even know if he actually was a share broker or that flat was his or even if he was actually the Gobi she loved. In a nutshell she wasn't prepared at all. That was too early.

"I... I... I have ordered dinner for the two of us tonight." He chuckled.

"Oh my god Gobi! So much for that..." She brushed his cheeks and he laughed.

"You are such a devil."

"Thank you."

"You wouldn't be sitting just like that if I was a devil." He said with a sly smile that changed the ambience suddenly.

"So... What would happen to me?" She had started to drift in the direction that she did not want to or maybe she was unknowingly craving for the same somewhere deep within!

"I would have consumed you and taken you to the formidable abyss." His voice became deeper as he shifted closer to her.

Shalu somehow had no intention to resist him. She sank deeper in him and said, "I want to be consumed."

She had never thought of seeing the first love of her life. First remains first, no matter what, and this one was forcibly removed from her life. He was locked safely in the most unreachable corner of her heart!

There had not been a day when she had not thought of him. Her feelings for him had not faded even by a shade. *Out of sight, out of mind* was a proverb that she laughed at proudly all her life.

He went closer between her legs and pulled her face towards himself. She kept the coffee mug right beside her on the slab and gave in immediately.

His breath was filled with her redolence as she started breathing heavily. Their wheezes mingled as he brushed her supple lips with his. Hormonal gushes were at the peak!

The lips parted and their tongues wrestled laudably as they both hugged each other and continued for minutes. Shalu was not an amateur; she had had numerous flings and Govind was highly equipped with all the necessary weapons! However, he was being careful enough. He did not want anything to go astray as that would waste all his efforts!

Shalu wrapped her legs around his waist and he picked her up from the slab. The coffee mug fell crashing down the floor and broke into pieces, but they didn't give a shit. They continued kissing as he turned around and pinned her against the wall.

He slid down and kissed her neck as she moaned. He plucked the buttons of her shirt from his teeth one by one, while moving down and smooching the smooth skin in her cleavage.

She enjoyed thoroughly and carped loudly as he bit her right shoulder.

"Easy Gobi..."

"Devil won't go easy. You are a sinner!" He winked.

"Yes... I am a sinner and I am going to sin more." She played along intensely.

"And so, shall you be punished." His voice was dense.

"I am your prisoner." Shalu did not know what had gotten into her. She had never experienced that kind of horniness ever. She wondered if Govind had turned out to be too much for her!

He soon carried her to the other side of the kitchen to avoid any bits and pieces of the broken coffee mug and put her on the slab.

He looked at her peach shirt that was then dropping from one side, revealing her red velvet bra and milky white shoulder. The bite already looked redder!

He looked into her deep eyes and then at her body.

"What... haa...?" Shalu caught him staring at her curves.

"You don't question the devil!" He bit her earlobe hard.

"Aaaah...!" She yelped, "You are so bad!"

"You dared to call me bad?"

"Yessss...." She hissed, "You are very bad!"

He bit her again and rustled, "The pot of your sin is full. You need to be chastised."

"Please chastise me." She was drunk in sensuality.

"Yes... There is no way out for you." He said, bent down and came up with a sharp broken piece of coffee mug and touched it on her face.

She said nothing and closed her eyes as he brushed it from her neck down towards her breast.

"Aaaaah.... Aaaaaah...." She yapped as he scratched her pap with the sharp piece in his hand.

She felt the pain and a lot of pleasure. She didn't care even if he skinned her! He moved down unclothing her and grazing her sensually.

A few seconds passed before all hell broke loose for her! Govind dropped his pants and pushed his shaft inside her. She cried with pleasure as she felt judders at the abyss and underwent a massive orgasm within minutes. But he didn't stop! She felt some pain for a minute and then she was again on top of the mountain enjoying the colossal blows that increased exponentially within minutes.

The ambience was overwhelmed by loud groans of a man and woman at the peak of pleasure as he clenched his teeth to release while pushing it further. She clasped him with all her might and quivered fervidly as the extreme tension from all the parts of her body was emancipated in less than a second.

The next moment he dismounted himself and lay beside her breathing heavily. He turned towards her after a few minutes and said with a smile, "See, I told you that a lot can happen over a cup of coffee."

She hugged him and said, "Indeed..."

"I missed you Shalu... a lot."

"I too missed you a lot."

That was the longest night in their lives and yet the shortest one! They made love the whole time until she left for the office the next morning with red eyes, plenty of love bites, wild scars everywhere and memories for a lifetime. It was all pleasure the previous night, but the new day was defined by agonizing pain all across her body. He did and made her do unimaginable things that whole night!

***

Govind dialled a number few minutes after Shalu left and said with a smile, “It worked extremely well.”

The voice on the other side said, “Do not lose your focus. You have more work to do.”

“Yup.” He replied and disconnected the call!

I feel so weary

12 February 2019
(Tuesday, 11:38 AM)

The effects of the absolutely happening previous night started taking a toll on Shalu as the day turned older. She felt drained both physiologically and psychologically and was unable to focus on anything whatsoever. She finally got the chance to call Govind after a gruesomely boring presentation by a couple who wanted to start a new cafeteria in her office building. She did not hear a single word uttered by them.

He took the call after a few rings, "Hello..."

"Hey Gobi! What's up?"

"Nothing... Just donated some money to the needy in the share market."

"Ha ha... Nice way to say that you suffered loss." Shalu was amused at his sense of humour.

He chuckled in reply and asked, "What are you doing?"

"I am missing you!" Shalu said straightforwardly.

"Whoa... really?"

"Of course! Do you need proof?"

"Yes... It sounds unpractical for a bigshot like..."

Shalu jumped in between and said, "Just shut up and tell me if you are free?"

"I am always free. For you, madame..." He replied.

"Okay then, I will see you in an hour."

"But don't you have work to do?" Govind shot back.

"Tell me if you don't want to meet..."

"I am waiting."

"Okay, I am coming." She said and disconnected.

Two hours later

"Coffee?" Govind asked while strapping a towel around his waist.

Shalu had reached his flat in less than forty-five minutes of her call and the two physically devastated, but extremely hungry souls didn't lose a moment to become one. Shalu was least bothered about how much her body hurt; all she cared for was conquering the uncharted territory with her beloved. They had gone for two straight rounds before their bodies gave up.

"Nope! Do you have Scotch or Beer?" She asked while putting herself inside Govind's t-shirt.

"I have both."

"Okay then, Scotch."

"I will be back in two minutes." He said, kissing her lips.

Shalu was busy enjoying Govind's cologne in his t-shirt when he stepped in with the drinks in his hands and they started chit-chatting about their past life that was mostly focussed on their post-separation. However, Shalu realised in a little while that it was only she who had been speaking and asked, "Don't you have anything to share Gobi?"

"You have had a great life Shalu. Nothing like my life..." His eyes articulated a thousand non-verbal emotions packed in the last four words; and Shalu thought she understood all of that, when she was quite heedless; regarding the past, the present and the future!

"I love you Gobi." Those three magical words left her lips routinely as if she had been saying it to him every day for the past decade. Shalu had never thought she would utter those words first. But that happened because she was intoxicated with his love. A love that had been inside her for years!

"I love you too Shalu." Govind replied and they hugged each other.

A few minutes passed when Shalu felt some weird inebriation taking over her.

"Gobi... I... I feel... I feel so weary." Shalu's voice suddenly turned slurry.

"What happened?" Govind asked her, looking into her eyes.

"I don't know." She said, rubbing her forehead, "My head feels weird and everything around me is spinning!"

"Ohh... Hmm...!" He continued, "I think... You are drugged."

"Wh... Wha..."

"These roofies are quite good. Didn't think it would work this fast!" He said with a sinister smile.

Shalu knew about the date rape drugs. She just didn't expect it to be used on her, especially by Govind, the one person whom she had loved since forever with all her heart!

"Bu.. But.. Why?" She was shocked, backstabbed mercilessly and hurt and drugged; and all of that combined together made it literally impossible for her to talk.

"Because it's revenge time honey!" He continued cynically, "Your loving father, Seth Manek Lal killed my parents and made me suffer so much that I yearned for a place as sweet as hell. Now baby, it's time he pays for all the sins of his past!"

"I... don't bee...live..." Darkness engulfed her before she could have completed the sentence.

I am not alone

12 February 2019
(Tuesday, 08:32 PM)

Shalini regained consciousness late in the evening. Sun had already bid good-bye and she looked around dazed, confused and irritated as her brain reminded of things that had transpired before she passed out. It took her a few more minutes to realise that she was in an alien bed in an unknown room. She turned extremely anxious and tried to get up, but her body failed her. A severe headache and body ache accompanied by extreme nausea shattered her body and her mind. She massaged her head sturdily to find some relief while trying to derive some sense of things around her. However, her mind still seemed fucked up after being roofied, although mildly, and failed to help her!

"So, you are up!" An unfamiliar voice made her stutter and she tried to run away when the same voice ricocheted in her ears again, "Careful or you will hurt yourself."

That someone caught her from behind to prevent her from falling. However, Shalu shrugged with all her might assuming it to be Govind without even opening her eyes and shouted, "Get the hell off me you bastard!"

"Easy, easy..." The voice echoed again, "The bastard you are talking about isn't here!"

It was then that Shalini identified that it was a female voice and struggled to open her eyes. It seemed like she had hit a sturdy wall with her head and the bricks of that wall had landed inside her head, budging around and hitting every corner painfully!

"Lay still..." The lady said again with utmost care and caressed her forehead.

"Who... who... are you...?" Shalu asked after a minute.

"I am Kanika."

"Who Kanika? I don't know any Kanika." She said and realized that she was blabbering nonsense and said, "Sorry... I am Shalini. Where am I? How did I reach here? My head hurts so bad?" Shalini said and started massaging her head forcefully again!

Kanika replied softly, "We are in Suyash's place. You were unconscious when a man put you here."

Shalini jumped out of bed with a big jerk and said, "That someone was Govind. The jerk drugged and kidnapped me!"

The next moment she fell back down with a thud and her stomach started behaving creepily. She turned extremely nauseous and looked around hurriedly to locate the washroom.

Kanika understood and assisted her to the location where she continued to dump everything loudly for the following few minutes.

***

"Can I get some water please?" She said sitting on the edge of the bed with Kanika's help after a few more minutes of struggle. The puke had used up every bit of energy that her body had stored up for emergencies!

"Just relax! I will get it for you." Kanika replied and walked to the refrigerator. She took out a bottle of water and gave it to her.

She sipped in bit by bit, trying to loosen up and asked her, “Why are you here and why are you being so kind to me?”

Kanika replied, “Because even I was kidnapped and put here before you, because of that son of a bitch Suyash, whom I fell so madly in love with.” The tone clearly suggested that she was in dire need to vent out her anger and despair!

Shalini was surprised at the coincidence and said, “And I am here because of Govind!”

Kanika, who seemed shocked at the coincidence whispered in despair, “So, the two of us are here because of some fucking boys.” and continued after a brief pause, “I don’t know if this is some kind of gang that works schematically.” She did her best to veil the dread in her heart to ensure that Shalini who wasn’t fully conscious until then did not switch to complete panic mode.

Her effort however seemed to be in vain as Shalini turned shakily instantly.

“But that idea seems vague as I did not find any type of gang here in the last few days that I have been here!” She tried to cover up before continuing angrily, “Although, I did find a nice fictional story that can be adapted for the silver screen.”

Shalini fell back down on the bed and sighed in relief, “Ohh!”

Although, she wasn’t fully convinced, her body needed to get rid of the drug. She continued massaging her head when Kanika said, “I think you should hydrate and get some rest for now... We can talk later!”

* * *

Three hours, six glasses of water and seven rounds of pee later!

“Damn! I never thought I would get roofied!” Shalini sat up straight after having a light dinner that had turned cold.

"Hmm... I know it feels awful to have been backstabbed by your own boyfriend!" Kanika had tears in her eyes.

Shalini hugged her, "Don't you worry. We will get out of this and teach those assholes a lesson for life."

Kanika hugged back and sobbed, "I don't know about you, but I am here because of my stupidity. I should have known that there cannot be a man as perfect as Suyash without an agenda. I have been such a fool, rather so blind in love that I was unable to see anything beyond."

"Means?" Shalini asked.

"Forget it, I am damn angry at myself. These thoughts just make me feel more miserable. Tell me about you." Kanika replied while wiping her tears and nose with a tissue paper kept on the table.

"My story is by far the same as yours."

"What...? As in...?" The words diverted all of Kanika's attention from herself towards her companion.

"I too am here because of my foolishness. I now realize how easy I was for him. Damn!" Shalini ground her teeth and continued, "It just took him a day dammit! How could I be such a fool?" And she thumped her feet on the ground.

"Just a day?" Kanika's mouth went wide open and she thought, "You really were very easy!"

"Don't start with me now, please. You have no idea of my journey. Moreover, he drugged me," Shalini said.

"Okay... Sorry." Kanika apologized immediately; although she did not mean it. She still believed that a day was too short a period.

"You know what, Govind says that my parents killed his parents and destroyed his life, which is practically impossible. I know them too well to accept his allegations." Shalini paused momentarily, "And now that I speak of it; everything seems very filmy!"

"So... Govind... But I don't understand how? Was it a fling that trapped you or what?"

"A fling wouldn't have had a chance to drug me dammit!" Shalini replied sarcastically, "Govind was my childhood love. He is the person I have never been able to get over. But now I really doubt if he is that person. My Gobi would never do this to me." She had tears in her eyes and acute sense of loathing for herself for her inanity.

Kanika however was shocked and exclaimed, "How is that even possible?" Her mind was hovering over the shocking revelations made by her accomplice and started working at its four hundred percent capacity. She could not help but wonder, "How was it possible that she was in a room with a girl whose so-called boyfriend had put the exact same allegations against her parents as her so-called boyfriend about on her?"

"How is what possible?" Shalini went to a high alert mode immediately.

She replied, "Suyash said... Umm... no... actually his uncle said the same to me."

"What did he say?" Shalini grew more and more suspicious with every passing moment.

"That my parents killed his parents and destroyed his life," Kanika said in a single breath.

"What? I mean are you saying this to me in real?" She was shocked.

"Yes!" Kanika looked straight at her and the two pairs of eyes opened wider with shock and dread.

Fright in Shalini's mind took form of words and she spilled it out while trembling, "Damn! Does this mean that we are stuck with a pair of psychos? Maybe nothing of the sort might have happened and they victimized us for the sake of their pleasure or maybe money or maybe something more!"

"You may be right. Fuck!" Kanika started hovering around in the room restlessly.

"I had even started to believe that bastard. I feel so damn guilty now. I am so sorry dad!" She then looked into Kanika's eyes and said, "We need to get out of this place."

People develop unexpected teams with strangers in dire situations; so did the two frightened souls who were not even aware of each other's existence until a few hours ago. They had suddenly turned into a solid support system for one another! That's nothing but a survival instinct that can lead to unprecedented outcomes!

"Yes, but how? Kanika looked back into Shalini's eyes and said with crippled confidence, "I have been here for the last couple of days and haven't been able to step out of this door."

"A couple of days and you did not try to escape?" Her confidence seemed boosted by the presence of an ally.

"Nope, because I was alone and damn frightened. Don't judge me!" She rolled her eyes.

"Sorry, I am not judging you. I thought you might have some intel!" Shalini started talking like a spy working for RAW who got captured by an enemy state.

"Intel... As in?" Kanika asked a bit confused by her sudden transformation and thought, "The roofies might still be at work."

"As in..." Shalini paused to think for second. "Do you know how many of them stay here?"

Kanika replied, "I have only seen Khalid, the caretaker of this house, who stays here regularly. Apart from that Suyash had come only one day and I saw another man, probably Govind, who put you here this evening."

"That means Khalid is usually alone here, right?"

"Yeah! I think so, everyone else comes and goes. I can see through that." Kanika said and pointed towards one of the windows.

"That's great!" Shalini asked excitedly, "So, this Khalid. Is he young and strong?"

"No... He is middle aged, lean and thin. I think we can take care of him together." Shalini's words enthused her.

"Okay... So, when does he come?"

Kanika replied, "He steps in with food three times a day, apart from occasional snacks. He also comes to clean the room once in the morning before bringing the breakfast."

"Then, I suppose we can take him down tomorrow morning?" Shalu asked.

"Yup!"

The Great Escape

13 February 2019
(Wednesday, 08:50 AM)

"May I come in?" Khalid knocked.

Shalini replied, "Yes please."

He unlatched the door from the outside and entered with a tray full of eatables.

The girls had been waiting for that moment. They had rehearsed and re-rehearsed the act several times to ensure nothing went wrong.

Kanika jumped on him from behind and pushed him to the ground as the tray flew off and everything splattered on the floor. Even Shalu joined the action immediately and it did not take them much time or effort to overpower him. They tied him to the chair, strapped his mouth and took the bunch of keys in his pocket before stepping out of the house. Lady luck was on their side and they found no one else. Moreover, Kanika had already spotted Suyash leaving the premises early that morning!

* * *

Ten minutes later

It seemed that luck favoured them only until they set their feet outside the periphery of that house and the two girls seemed to be lost even before they started.

They stared at the road that seemed to touch heaven on either side, clueless. The sun was already dropping heat missiles even though it was just nine in the morning! They started walking towards a direction that appeared to be their best guess.

"Why is it so hot even at nine?" Kanika complained looking at her watch and wiping the sweat beads off her brow with her forefinger.

"It's hot all year round here Kanika!" Shalini said and asked after a moment, "Are you sure you know where we are going?"

"Nope, I am not very sure. It was already dark when I came here, but I think national highway should be some thirty minutes' drive from here."

"Shit! A thirty minutes' drive could mean anywhere from twenty to fifty kilometres. How the fuck are we supposed to reach there?" Shalini was already struggling to breathe. Although she had been working out regularly, the drug that her body was working hard to get rid of through perspiration and excretion seemed to be taking a toll on her.

"You are right, but tell me if you have any other way. I can't even see any fucking vehicle to get us a lift."

"Yeah, but at least we should be moving in the right direction." Shalini said sarcastically while exerting herself through every step.

"I think we are." Kanika rolled her eyes.

The two lonesome girls continued walking through the ten feet wide unmaintained pitched road that divided the massive span of unending and uncultivated fields into two parts. There wasn't a soul around them, not even of animals and the only good that the road offered was the reflection of heat at a multiplied intensity.

They walked under the scorching sun for more than an hour, but found nothing. None of them were used to enduring those conditions and sat down by the road after the next few minutes; dehydrated and whacked.

"I think it was a bad idea to leave the house."

"I agree. Let's go back." Shalini, who was in a worse condition replied while trying to get hold of her body.

"If only we could find someone who could help us. Please god..." This time it was Kanika who sought divine help through prayer and it seemed that god answered her instantaneously. They saw a vehicle nearing them speedily and Shalini ran to the middle of the road and started waving, "Stop... help... please help...!" Kanika joined her immediately and the car came to a halt with a loud screech.

A man stepped out amongst the clouds of dust and Kanika shouted at the top of her voice the moment her eyes caught sight of the being, "Fuck... Shalini run... It's them!"

The next thirty minutes comprised of those men strapping the sapped ladies, putting them in the car and bringing them back to the place from where they had tried to make the great escape!

Does she know him?

Two days later...

Newton's third law states, *To every action, there is an equal and opposite reaction!*

Things changed drastically after that day. Khalid, the keeper, who had been taking very good care of their needs did that no longer. As a matter of fact, he was vexed and would have slapped the girls every time he saw them if that was allowed. The look in his eyes said it all. Moreover, he intentionally made the food crappy for them by adding extra or no salt, spices, chillies, etc., and visited them only to serve food three times a day. Even then, he was always accompanied by a six feet tall, sturdy middle-aged man with big moustaches who looked like a ruthless villain of some C-grade movie!

The biggest woe for the girls was that they were separated and incarcerated in different rooms to prevent them from making any that kind of attempt in future. In addition, two other men were placed, who moved hither and tither within the premises of the house twenty-four hours a day.

They had lost all privileges except for shitty, but timely meals!

****

Shalu was lying on the bed, wetting the pillow with her tears when Govind stepped in uninvited. His entry pushed her to an untimely panic mode and she yelled at the top of her voice, "What the fuck do you think you are doing Govind?"

He ignored her as if she was both invisible and inaudible and directed the person with him to place the forty-two-inch LED television where he wanted it.

"Dammit! What the fuck is this?" She was confused and shouted again and he snubbed her again, still enacting to be busy in the placement of the device.

"I don't need any entertainment. Take this fucking TV out of here."

"You are going to like it." Govind uttered the first sentence of the day with a sly smile.

"Just go away you fucking criminals!" Shalu continued yelling in panic mode, but her words did not go unnoticed then. Govind took out a pistol and put it on her forehead immediately, "Shhh... Just shut the hell up!"

Shalu had not expected that and was shaken to the soul. She however geared up and said, "Kill me if you want to or just let me go."

"Don't worry, I will grant your wish." Govind sneered wickedly waving the weapon in his hand.

She turned silent contemplating what wish he was about to grant? Killing or freeing? She was too afraid to speak after that and watched them spitefully as they completed the installation. The other person left the room soon after!

"Was that Suyash?" She asked.

"That's none of your business." He answered coldly.

"What is it you want Govind?"

"I want to watch a movie with you." Govind said with a cold smile.

She looked at him; it wasn't the sweet genuine smile that she had seen until recently; rather it was a scary one! She turned restless with countless apprehensions as he inserted a pen drive and switched on the TV.

And damn! The biggest fear of her life stared straight into her soul like a giant wolf ready to devour her into pieces. Her eyes went wide open as the movie started to play. There were multiple videos of them making love with an exception that Govind's identity was completely hidden!

"What the fuck Govind? How could you? You bastard!" She shouted and slapped him, *Baaam... baaam... baaam...*

He smiled in reply and said sarcastically, "Happy now baby?"

All the torture in the jail made those slaps feel like a gentle pat to him.

"I loved you from the core of my heart dammit and you did this to me." She started crying outrageously, "But I suppose you are not the Govind that I knew once upon a time!"

Govind gave her a minute to mourn and then whispered right in to her ear, "Enough of the drama honey. Now listen to me carefully; this video contains everything that a lot of people would love to see and feel." He winked ignoring her tears and continued coldly, "If you don't want it to go viral you are going to do what I tell you."

She was shattered. She didn't know what to think or say. Her hands and feet were already cold. The world around her started spinning uncontrollably and she fell down on her knees. She knew she had to be strong, but her mind and body had already given up.

She wanted to hang herself or jump out of the window or slash her wrists or do anything that could take her out of that. She knew that she was in a big shit hole and the only way to survive (if she wanted to survive) was to abide by his words then.

Devoid of all options, she started weeping vigorously while thumping the floor with her palms.

"No...no... no... Govind you can't do this to me. Please don't do this to me. I beg of you." She continued pleading for minutes. However, Govind, who seemed absolutely untouched by her words and tears said frigidly, "So, are you going to do what I tell you?"

Shalini realised that she was wasting herself on the most callous heart known and spurted brashly, "What the fuck do you want dammit? Just tell me!"

"That's like a good girl." He said and dialled a number. A phone rang in the adjacent room and he said, "Now bring her here."

"Okay, sir." The person on the other side said and disconnected and Govind walked out of the room.

***

"The two of you can share the room for some time now." A person brought Kanika and stepped out. The two weary girls looked at each other. They had identical looks. Their faces were lifeless with gigantic inscriptions of anxiety all across. Their eyes were enflamed by reason of intense crying and tears refrained from dripping.

"How could he do this to me?" Shalu said and hugged Kanika and both of them started sobbing like never before. The waters in their eyes seemed to break a gargantuan dam, flooding each other's dress. They needed a shoulder to cry and the two shattered ladies found that in each other!

Kanika asked, "Videos?"

Shalu replied, "Yes!" and continued, "I loved him dammit! I loved him since my childhood days. We were never in touch. I was never able to move on with anybody in the US or anywhere else in the world, that was my love for him. I don't know why my heart was always fixed on him and he turned out to be the biggest mistake of my life. I hate him. I so hate him!"

"Me too!" It was then Kanika's turn, "I thought that he loved me. Everything was a fucking lie. And I think we became victims of some sex racketeers."

Shalu started blabbering in fluster, "Dammit! I am finished now. I know that I am finished. I don't want to live anymore." and she seemed asphyxiated.

Kanika started rubbing her back and patting her cheeks, "Shalu... Shalu... Get yourself together... Please don't lose yourself. I need you."

***

It took Kanika some time and effort to pull her accomplice back to normalcy, but she was successful.

She then said after a few minutes, "But there is one thing that I still don't understand."

Shalu tried to get her head back in to the situation and asked, "What?"

"They have our video and could have easily blackmailed us over the phone or mail or any other mode of communication. Then why the hell are we here?"

"I don't know... maybe they have some buyers for us." Shalini uttered some of the most horrifying words.

"You better be wrong." Kanika was shaken at the mere thought of it when somebody unlatched the door from outside.

"Dammit! Are the buyers already here?" Shalini turned pale. However, it was the same person who had brought Kanika.

She said sarcastically, "See! Your Suyash is here."

"He isn't Suyash." Kanika said with surprise.

"I don't care who you are mister." Shalini suddenly lost her cool and shouted at the top of her voice, "Just tell us why we are here?"

"He knows nothing. I have the answers." The voice turned their eyes towards the entrance and Shalini who was facing the door shouted instantly, "Just give us the fucking answers Govind...!"

Even Kanika turned around instinctively and exclaimed, "But... But... He is Suyash...!"

The two ladies looked at each other in bewilderment trying to digest the reality that teased them like a mischievous monkey swinging on the highest branch of the tallest tree after stealing the priceless from them. They knew what happened to them as the man looked into Kanika's eyes and reinforced the fact, "Yes babe, I am your Suyash."

He then turned towards Shalini and said in continuance, "... and your Govind!"

I can hear my papa

Shalu was still trying to assimilate what had unravelled in the last few minutes while Kanika murmured to herself continually, "How can you be such a fool Kanika? This man is nothing that you thought him to be. He is just a cheat, a thug and you gave him everything you had. How can you be so stupid?"

Kanika had always been super confident regarding her choices, but the fact that she didn't even know the real identity of the person with whom she had been so madly in love with was too much for her to bear! Her heart had already broken, but then it was smashed and then burned and then again ground to cellular level!

However, the two girls over there were no good-for-nothing, weak human beings who could be demolished akin to a sand castle. Moreover, they were two!

Shalu, although hurt and baffled, sensed that Kanika was losing herself. Kanika had lifted her up earlier and she knew then that it was her turn. She said to her, "C'mon Kanika, we cannot be weak now. Stop crying and get the fuck up. We cannot let this asshole win."

Shalini did not say anything outstanding, but simple words can sometimes work magic and it did! It made Kanika realise that she was acting as if she'd already been beaten and she was not the kind of lady who could go down without a fight. She pulled herself together, wiped her eyes, put a determined look on her face and said sternly, "Yesssss.... So, Mr Suyash... aka Mr Govind... aka Mr Stinking Asshole... You have what you wanted. You fucked us and you have our videos. Now tell us what the hell are we doing here?"

"What are you ready to do for the answers Kanika?" The multiple-named man said immediately while looking into her eyes with a sinister smile that was intended to take her soul; and it did. Kanika was shaken inside out.

Shalu apprehended and got in between the two and said, "Anything you bastard..."

"If that's the case; let's talk to your dad." He said and slipped his hands in to his pocket as if taking out cell phone.

"Shit... No..." Shalu yelled reflexively at the top of her voice, "He will kill me." His words made her quiver in fear instantly.

"Tch tch! And someone claimed to do anything..." He said mockingly, "Let me ask you the same question differently... Are you willing to die?" He laughed, thoroughly enjoying her dire state and ensured making it worse by fidgeting with his phone.

Shalini assumed he would be calling her father and said trembling, "Please don't call him; please!"

He hushed her. "Shh! It is going to happen baby. Now, I can either talk to him in front of you, in which case even you will get to speak to him, or you can continue with your niggling and I will go out.

Shalini wisely chose the former. She was confident that her father would find and take them out of that mess in no time.

She realised that was her only chance and said, "Ok, I won't utter a word."

"Good girl!" He said and dialled a number.

"Hello..." Seth Manek Lal took the call immediately, contrary to his general habit of waiting up to six or seven rings. Even his voice seemed different.

She started screaming the moment she recognised her father's voice, "Papa... I am here outside Raipur. Govind has kidnapped me." but her volume reduced manifolds as she saw the multi-named person smiling peacefully and derisively, "Please call the police. Save me papa." The excitement in her face was replaced by confusion and fright as he gave her the phone.

"Dad?" She said with a big question mark on her face because his voice was audible even without the phone. It meant that he was somewhere in that building, probably outside the room and Shalini shouted in excitement, "I can hear you papa," and rushed out of the room.

She let out a deep breath of relief the moment her eyes found him right in front of her. She hugged him tight and the ocean of tears that she had managed to keep in check for the past few minutes flowed out like an unstoppable tsunami.

However, Sethji did not exhibit synonymous emotions and pushed her away forcefully. She looked at him in perplexity before a heavy slap fell on her cheek at lightning speed, *Baaam!*

Shalini had her question answered and she knew that she deserved that entire wrath. She dropped her head as he screamed at the top of his voice while shaking in anger, "You bitch, you did not find anyone else except for this roadside dog."

"It is not her fault, don't hit her." An unfamiliar voice of a Nepali man standing next to Sethji hit Shalini's ears. He then pointed towards the multi-named being and said, "It's that filthy dog that needs to be blamed!"

Kanika who was still inside recognized her father's voice and rushed outside shouting at the top of her voice, "Dad!" and hugged him tight!

Sins of the past

Shalini cried in agony and jealousy as Mr Chettri hugged her daughter. Kanika cried fervidly against his chest. Shalini had expected the same love and understanding from her father, but he had already failed her, like always!

She looked into her dad's eyes that fumed with rage and said wordlessly, "I know all that you did."

Just then Govind aka Suyash stepped out of the room and Sethji roared in anger, "Who the hell you think you are, you bastard? How dare you touch my daughter? Do I need to remind you what I am capable of?"

"I know what you are capable of Sethji. Your daughter's life is in jeopardy and you still talk about your power." He smirked.

Sethji looked into his eyes and said, "I should have killed you along with your family or with your friends that day. It was my mistake. But don't worry, I am going to make sure you die this time!"

Shalini, who was already going through an intense emotional turmoil was absolutely stunned by her father's words.

"That's what I wanted your daughter to hear Sethji. She wasn't ready to believe that you actually killed someone's whole family." He fumed, "However, what I did not tell her was how you made that someone suffer for years until finally taking that someone's life."

Shalini wanted to ask out loud, "What is all of this papa?" But the jolt had paralysed her temporarily.

"Yes... You dared to touch my daughter and hamper my reputation. I could not have allowed you even a drop of happiness in this life." Manek Lal said arrogantly. And then, suddenly his eyes went wide open as if he had set foot on a coin that was jinxed to take his life. He said boggled, "Wait... You just said that *you told her that I killed someone's family and made that someone suffer until finally taking that someone's life.* Who the fuck are you? Are you not Govind?"

"No Sethji. You got it right. I am not Govind."

Shalu had already assumed until then that that man could not have been Govind and yelled, "I knew it..! My Gobi could have never done this to me!"

While Manek Lal asked flabbergasted, "Then who the fuck are you and where the hell is Govind? I did not kill him; because I wanted him to suffer every second in this life!"

"It happened exactly how you wanted Mr Manek Lal. He suffered every moment until he died!" He radiated nothing but abhorrence, "And I am the guy that your man shot twice that day and left to die. I am Rishab."

"Do you mean that Govind is dead?" The words hardly left Shalini's strangled throat.

"Unfortunately, yes!" Rishab turned towards her and said with hatred, sympathy and dejection, "Courtesy your father!"

Shalu got down on her knees with a thud and started howling inconsolably! Destiny had given her the long-lost love and then snatched it away nastily! Kanika reached out and tried to tend to the bereft soul unsuccessfully.

However, Seth Manek Lal didn't seem to care about anything and said callously, "But I didn't kill him."

"Wow! Amazing!!!" Rishab clapped sarcastically and continued, "Yes, you are right. You did not kill him. But you took away every reason for him to live. You broke his bones and then burnt his parents alive in front of his eyes when he was just a kid; then you made his life a living hell in the mental asylum and the prison; and then when he was just trying to live a little with us, his only friends you tried to kill. Period. You actually killed everyone he loved right in front of his eyes. You left the place saying you were never going to let him be happy dammit! You left him no choice. Suyash's head was splattered into pieces and your men had pierced two bullets in my chest and left me in the pool of my blood. All he knew was that we were gone and he blamed only himself for the death of his only friends. So, what did he do? He slashed his wrists right then!"

"But how is it possible? You look so much like Govind." Shalu uttered those words with utmost difficulty amidst bitter sobs! She still hoped that her Gobi was alive and he was doing all of that just to get his revenge from her father.

"That's because of plastic surgery." Rishab replied, "Not much had to be done. Fortunately, we shared a lot of features."

"But how the hell did you survive after those two bullets? You must be one heck of a tough man!" Manek Lal overlooked his daughter's agony and interrupted him coldly.

"There are basically two reasons. Firstly, because destiny wanted me to live so that I could make a couple of people pay for the sins of their past and secondly because of the untiring labour and care of him!" Rishab said pointing towards Rashid Ijaz, "Rashid uncle came home soon after you left and took us to the hospital where Suyash and Govind were declared dead on arrival. I, however, had to undergo multiple surgeries before I got back to normalcy after months."

"Ohh... I am so sorry for what you had to undergo because of me; but I will ensure that even you are declared *dead on arrival* this time, along with this old man!" Sethji shouted and took out a pistol from his pocket and pointed it right to his face, "Now tell me what good would that video do to you if I kill you right now?"

"Don't be a fool Sethji. You are not talking to the helpless Govind who watched his parents being burned alive right in front of his eyes; neither are you talking to a weak child whom you ensured being tortured first in the mental asylum and then in the jail through your contacts; and neither are you talking to an unprepared Govind in front of whose eyes you killed his best friends just to ensure that he thought a million times before smiling." He said with a smile, "You are in my house now!"

"Your house?" Manel Lal laughed mockingly, "I am going to kill everyone here and then put you back to the jail where you came from and there's nothing you can do about it."

Rishab started laughing monstrously in response and was immediately joined by Rashid!

"Have you lost your mind?" Sethji was a bit bewildered.

"Nope, I was just amused by your words. I know you are roaring because you think your men will drop in anytime by the help of the tracker in your phone and your car."

"Wh... What... do you mean..?" Sethji stammered. He knew he was busted and screwed.

"I mean that the tracker from your phone and car was removed by your own secretary before you left your place. Not only that, he also switched off the location of your phone."

"Bu... bu... But... ho...!" Manek Lal was at a loss of words.

"Because, he was there when you and your men battered the little kid Govind until all the bones in his body broke. And then he witnessed first-hand how you murdered his entire family mercilessly. And yet again, he knew all that you did to him later! He wishes so much to go back in time and at least try to stop you from committing those heinous crimes; but that isn't possible." Rishab continued after a sigh, "His heart was filled with tremendous guilt that had haunted him for years and then I approached him with a cheque. But he tore it off and accepted to do everything that I wanted him to as he saw that as his only chance to redemption before meeting our maker."

"Bravo, what a plan!" Sethji announced acerbically while waving his gun, "I think all of you are in a hurry to meet your maker!"

"Don't be a fool Sethji. And also remember, you pull a trigger here and my friend here will press a button and everything will be available for the whole world to watch before you can imagine. Moreover, don't forget that all of these are my men." Rishab said uncaringly.

"You think I care about that fucking video anymore. I am going to kill this girl right now!" He said, pointed the gun towards Shalini and pulled the trigger immediately!

It was only due to Rishab's quick reflexive action that he shoved Sethji's hand away so that the bullet missed Shalini by a few inches before hitting the wall behind her. He then threw him to the ground and the ageing Manek Lal lost consciousness immediately. Two of the men who had ran down picked and strapped him to the chair.

However, Shalu was broken. She couldn't believe what had gone down. She had never thought even in her wildest dreams that her father would try to kill her. She realized how undervalued she was in his eyes. The series of sentimental mayhem seemed to get worse by every passing moment.

How could he try to kill me?

How could he burn Gobi's parents alive?

How could he kill so many people just like that?

The questions hurt her like a sword that had been pierced and was being continually swivelled in her body!

*****

The bullet episode had turned things a bit chaotic and Kanika's father who was standing there as a mute spectator had started shaking in terror.

"Please let my father go Rishab. See he is trembling in fear. Something may happen to him. I am sorry about what you and your friends had to undergo because of Seth Manek Lal. But we have nothing to do with it. Please let us go. At least please let him go." Kanika pleaded with folded arms.

Rishab looked into the eyes of Kanika's father and said, "Really Mr Komal Chettri, have you told anything to your daughter about the sins of your past?"

"So... son... I don't know what you are talking about. I am a simple man, nothing like Sethji. I don't have money or power. All I have is my daughter. This old man requests you. Please delete the video and don't let it go viral. I will give you whatever I have. I am just a middle class man, please son... please...!" Mr Chettri got down on his knees and started crying with folded hands.

Rishab and Rashid looked at each other as he continued pleading, "Why are doing this to us son? You have no idea of the torment you have made us undergo in the last few days."

Kanika was shocked, "Torment... last few days... as in? What are you saying papa?"

"They have been sending us your videos for quite a few days now... A new video every other day through a man who ensured we saw it every time by putting a gun on our temple." He started crying vigorously.

"Why didn't you tell me about it, papa?" Kanika joined her father in tears.

"For your own safety. They had warned us if we try to talk about it with you or anyone else, they would kill you and make the videos viral."

Kanika's heart was shattered at the disclosure, the pain that her parents had to undergo maddened her in anger. She tried to slap Rishab who caught her hand, twisted her and put the pistol on her temple and said, "Don't you dare!"

Her father, Mr Komal Chettri, went down prostrate and wailed, "Please leave her... please leave us. I beg of you."

"I don't want you to Mr Chettri aka Mr Komal Tamang..."

He looked up into Rishab's eyes. The name turned him into a corpse. His tears vanished and there was intense horror in his eyes.

"Yes Mr Komal Tamang. We know all about you." Rishab continued.

"I don't know what you are talking about?" Kanika's dad looked here and there.

"Is it? Then you won't even know about these." He threw the FIRs and the pics in the file and paper cuttings that contained his and his wife's pic.

He started shaking intensely.

"Don't throw these things at him dammit! I know that these are fake." Kanika's heart was not ready to accept that her father could have done anything that Rashid had told her earlier.

"He knows that it's not fake, just look into his eyes." Rashid said with a smouldering intensity and continued, "...but I have something else for you." He signalled and one of the men came in with an old lady on a wheel chair.

Rishab then walked close to her and went down on his knees with his palms on hers, "You know who she is?"

All the people in the room looked at the motionless lady clad in a white sari with pity.

Mr Chettri was dumbfounded the moment he saw her and started whining vehemently. Jiffy and he broke out vociferously, "I am so sorry."

Kanika was scandalised at his reaction.

"Yes Chettri Sahib... She is none other than Suyash's mother. The very same lady who had a perfect life and a perfect family until you came in and destroyed everything she had." Rishab caressed her head and rubbed her hands lovingly, "Her body is alive, but she is as good as dead. She has been in the mental asylum for years." He paused momentarily to wipe his tears, "This is what happens when a group of so-called men rip apart the dignity of a woman, make a video of it and sell it to sex mafias for money and then leave her to watch her husband die helplessly. You have no idea what you made her go through."

Chettri buried his head towards his chest with self-loathing and tears as Rishab continued, "Bhuvan, Suyash's uncle, who had promised to take care of her sister-in-law, threw her into a government mental asylum after the doctors diagnosed her with PTSD (Post Traumatic Stress Disorder), before leaving with Suyash. Not only that, he also told the child that his mother was dead and the bereaving Suyash had no option but to mourn his parent's death day and night. It was only later that Rashid uncle came into picture and put her into a good doctor's care who diagnosed that her condition had worsened. She suffered from Schizophrenia. She did not get any better with time and suffered a paralysis on the entire left side of her body after a few years due to a condition called Conversion Disorder!"

Rishab's words were followed by a pin drop silence for many seconds as Kanika stared at her father in disbelief.

"Why papa?" She was under tremendous agony and spoke with utmost difficulty.

Mr Chettri did not possess the courage to face her daughter replied face down, "I have no excuse beta. I and your mother were addicted to drugs and committed those crimes for cash. We could see nothing but money to get cocaine for ourselves."

Kanika listened to every word from her father's mouth sceptically as he continued, "However, what happened with Suyash's family was planned by Suyash's own uncle, Bhuvan. He visited and helped us out of the lockup after that accident and offered us an amount we could not have refused. In return, he just wanted us to kill his brother Niket, that is Suyash's father." Chettri paused for a breath, "But, we added our own agenda. Niket had caused us a loss and we took up that opportunity to make up for it through his own wife. So, we made the video that we had earlier planned to shoot with the girl who was saved by them."

"Damn! How could you do that papa?" Kanika broke down. "I am ashamed to be your daughter!"

"Please don't say it Kanika. You are my life. My everything!"

"So was Suyash to Niket and Bushra, and you destroyed them all. That too for money and drugs. Shame on you Mr Chettri!" That was the first time that Kanika had called her dad by his name.

"I am really sorry. Please forgive me." He went down on his knees and pleaded.

"You think a sorry is enough after what you made them go through. You don't have an inkling of what happened to Suyash after that!" Rishab jumped into the conversation immediately, "And how you see her now is nothing as compared to how you left her dammit!" Rishab pointed towards Bushra towards the end of sentence.

"I am so sorry... sorry... sorry... sorry!" Chettri cried continually.

***

"I am sorry for making you go through everything ladies, but I did what I had to do for what these monsters made Govind and Suyash go through." Rishab said while looking at Kanika and Shalini.

He then turned his gaze towards Shalu and said, "The only thing we didn't expect was Seth Manek Lal trying to kill his own daughter."

"I can't expect anything better from a person like him." Shalini who had recomposed herself to some extent until then said, "I hate him; he is such a monster. Damn! He even killed my Go...bi! I am so sorry Gobi." Her sobs penetrated the silence of the room once again.

A number of police men stepped into the house by the time she completed her sentence. Manek Lal, who had regained his consciousness until then started shouting while wriggling to free himself from the chair, "Yes...Yes... Thank god you are here inspector saab. Arrest these bastards! They abducted my daughter, tried to extort money from me and also tried to kill us all."

"Shhh... We know whom to arrest Sethji." The man with three shining stars on his khaki uniform hushed him and commanded, "Arrest Manek Lal and Komal Chettri."

"What the fuck? Don't you dare touch me." Sethji threatened the constable who neared him.

The inspector took the handcuffs from him and put it in Sethji's hands as he shouted, "You don't know how powerful I am you bastard!" He tried to shake him off, but the inspector's grip was just too much for him. Manek Lal then threatened him, "Now I am going to make even your life miserable inspector. You just signed a death warrant for yourself and your family." The police man seemed highly unconcerned so then Lal turned his attention towards Rishab and said, "And now I know your face too, you asshole. You are a dead man. You just don't know it yet!"

Rishab said sarcastically, "Shut the fuck up Manek Lal. None of your words matter now. Just think, how on earth do you think the cops came in and arrested you immediately?"

The words pushed Manek Lal to the brink of silence as he stared at him blankly. Rishab was right, Sethji hadn't thought that through!

Rishab then pointed at the number of small cameras and microphones that were fitted in various places all across the room and said calmly, "The Superintendent of Police happens to be a friend of Rashid uncle and he has a live feed of all that had happened here. Even the local police station from where all these khaki clad gentlemen arrived saw it all. Even the media will get hold of the video in due course; and of course that will be edited to suit our needs and fuck your whole life. This time you are not getting out Manek Lal."

Seth Manek Lal was dumbfound. That was the first time in forever that he was beaten and he knew it. So, he walked out silently with the policemen but whispered in Rishab's ears just as he crossed him, "All of you including that SP are going to suffer. Don't think that you won!"

"My friends were sinless roses when you crushed them mercilessly; and then when all of us tried to move on in life you came in and killed all of my friends for no reason. You called this upon yourself. Our lives have been a bed of thorns ceaselessly, where I have been forced to sleep night and day. Courtesy; people like you. But now it's your turn." Rishab said and shrugged his shoulder. "I am not afraid of pain anymore."

Epilogue

The court announced Seth Manek Lal and Komal Chettri aka Komal Tamang life imprisonment. Even Kanika and Shalini stood as witnesses against them. It was their move to loosen the guilt trap that had been squeezing the life out of them due to their parent's gory crimes!

Rishab, who had already resigned from his job at MNB bank a few days before executing the plan's final episode, secured another one in BYC Bank, England, soon after while still making a lot of money through share market. He was joined by Rashid and Bushra as he got himself settled in the new place.

***

The criminals detailed above had no right to know any more, but I cannot let all of you excellent readers keep wondering about Rishab's past, of course in brief. So, nobody around knew that he was a brilliant student and a class topper since the beginning before his whole family succumbed to a gruesome catastrophe. Subsequently, he was pushed into an orphanage where he stabbed a couple of *supposedly gullible* women unrelentingly until they stopped moving, resulting him landing in the Correction Centre!

However, Rashid Ijaz, who took up his responsibility after the death of his beloved nephew Suyash, sensed his intelligence in next to no time! He then rechristened him as Suyash for the sake of Suyash's mother and ensured that he got a good education before instigating the cerebrally planned revenge spree!

Further, Rishab (or Suyash) developed a strong affinity towards the share market and allied investments during his MBA, which also helped him secure one of the highest packages during the placements! His knowledge, dedication and hard work put him in the good books of the company soon after and fetched him the enviable position of the Marketing Head of the Central India within a very short span of time!

***

Anon, Kanika got herself transferred to the company's office in Malaysia. She did not want to stay anywhere near Raipur or Siliguri or even in India after undergoing the massive physical and psychological debacle.

On the other hand, Shalini drowned herself in work in her efforts to move on. She took control of Lal's Infra, the company started by her dad and did not leave even a stone unturned to undo the damage caused to the company's reputation after the entire fiasco.

Kanika and Shalini became best friends, but they never talked about the one guy who changed their lives forever!

***